Time Shifters
Into the Past

(Book One)

by

KATE FROST

LEMON TREE PRESS

Paperback Edition 2016

ISBN 978-0-9954780-1-5

Copyright © Kate Frost 2016

Cover design and map by Rachel Lawston.

Time Shifters
Into the Past

by

KATE FROST

LEMON
TREE
PRESS

For Leo

ROBBIE'S MAP

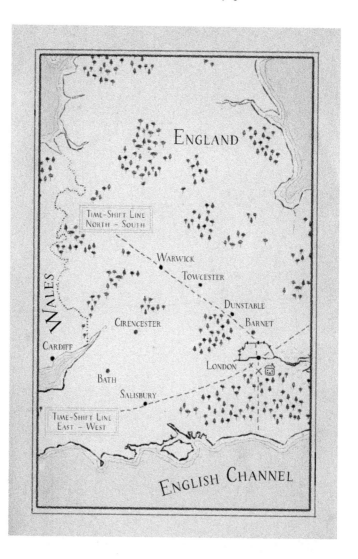

Chapter One

I knew something bad was going to happen the second we reached the castle.

"Not holding hands with your boyfriend then?" Lizzie Andrews said, knocking into me as she stalked past in her servant's costume and Nike trainers.

"Danny's my best friend, not my boyfriend. You know that," I called after her.

We walked beneath the iron teeth of Warwick Castle's portcullis and I glanced at Danny.

"Ignore her, Maisie," he said, as Lizzie giggled with her friends.

Emerging on the other side of the gatehouse was like stepping into another world. Everyone was dressed up in medieval costumes – the whole of my class and the guides who showed us around. We gathered on the pathway next to one of the tall stone towers before being split off into smaller groups by our history teacher, Miss Chard. As usual Lizzie and her two clone-like friends were in my group. We explored the outside of the castle first, missing out on the warmth of the log fire in the Great Hall. We walked along the ramparts and climbed more than five hundred steps to the top of Guy's Tower. Houses and trees stretched for miles in all directions, spreading away from the river and castle.

"Look at the knights, Danny!" I pointed to a

crowd that had gathered on the far side of the grass.

"Huh?" he replied, removing his earphones and snapping his mobile shut.

"This place is amazing." Leaning between stone turrets I watched two men in armour fight each other with swords.

"The stuff my grandad told me about what happened to him in World War II was pretty cool. This is old and boring."

"It's called history, Danny."

He sighed and put his mobile into his trouser pocket beneath his brown tunic. "Has it got a dungeon?"

"Yes."

"With prisoners chained to walls?"

"Maybe."

"And instruments of torture?"

"You're sick."

~

There was a castle dungeon with cobwebs and severed heads on spikes and actors made up to look diseased and bloodied who made everyone jump. Even Danny. A masked torturer displayed his tools: The Jaw Breaker, The Tongue Tearer and The Claw, which was used to rip, tear and dig into the prisoners' flesh. Lizzie and her friends, Josie and Megan, didn't make it past the Labyrinth of Lost Souls because a dark-hooded figure suddenly appeared in front of them and they ran back out of the dungeon screaming. Lizzie looked seriously pale like she was going to be sick. There were decaying bodies, scary chanting and an execution. It was the best bit, way more interesting than the richly decorated state rooms in the main part of the castle where we weren't allowed to touch anything.

Behind the dungeon entrance in the shadow of a large tree was the original castle gaol. A narrow flight of dimly lit stone steps disappeared through a hatch at the base of Caesar's Tower. I waited with Danny and made sure we were the last to go down. It was damp and cold below ground.

Danny paced across the gaol. "They could at least have had someone locked up in here."

An open drain ran across the middle of the stone floor. "It must have smelt bad," I said, wrinkling my nose at the thought of the unwashed prisoners having to use the dungeon as the toilet.

"Really disgusting. They probably had to sleep in their poo."

"Yuck."

"How many people died in here, do you think?"

"A lot."

"Their ghosts probably still haunt this place." Danny headed towards the steps. "I'm going back up. You coming, Maisie?"

"In a minute." I heard him run up the steps. I traced my fingers across the scratched stone walls and imagined the cries for help of starved prisoners alone in the dark. I shivered. Returning footsteps sounded on the steps and I walked towards the open doorway.

On the bottom step, white Nike trainers gleamed beneath the dark cloth of a skirt. I looked up at blonde hair falling across Lizzie's face. She folded her arms and glared at me. "What's so interesting down here?"

"Nothing." I tried to squeeze past her on the narrow steps but she grabbed the neck of my tunic-style dress and shoved me against the uneven stone wall. Her fingers dug into my shoulders and I winced.

"You've got no big brother to look after you today," she said. The dim light on the curved ceiling cast shadows over her grinning face. "I saw your boyfriend running out of here like a girl."

I felt the cold wall through the material of my costume. Each stone jabbed into my back. I sighed. "He's not my boyfriend."

"Then why do you follow him everywhere?"

"I don't."

"You so do."

"He's my friend."

"Yeah, *boyfriend*." She pressed against my shoulders. "You scared?"

"No more than you were in the dungeon."

She shoved me harder against the wall. "So how come you didn't dress up as a peasant today?"

I frowned. "I did."

"Really? Your mum must dress you up every day then."

"Why are you always so mean?"

"Are you crying?"

"You're hurting me." I couldn't stare her out any longer. I blinked back tears and glanced away from her pale, smirking face to the grey stone steps leading up to daylight. "Danny!" I shouted. "Miss Chard!"

Lizzie's grip tightened on my shoulders. "You're pathetic."

The clang of iron bars slamming shut made us jump. Lizzie's hands left my shoulders and grasped the wall on either side of me. The steps beneath my feet rumbled and shook. I felt stones shuffle against my back as the wall shifted. Dust from the cracks in the stone puffed into the air. The light above us flickered like a disco light before going out, plunging us into darkness. I couldn't see anything but it felt like I was spinning round and round, faster and faster. Then everything went quiet and the dizziness stopped as my back jolted against the stone wall. A sickening, rotten smell like a stink bomb hit me, oozing up from the dungeon below. My breath caught in my throat. Lizzie coughed and spluttered.

"Who's there?" a voice croaked from the darkness.

I froze. "There was no one down there," I whispered. I could see a square of inviting grey light at the top of the stairs.

Lizzie breathed fast. "What is this, some kind of freak show?" She pushed me hard against the wall, knocking my breath from me before running up the steps. I peered into the gloom and gasped. A thin, pale face smeared with dirt stared up at me. His skeletal fingers clutched at the bars of the gaol door.

"Help me," he pleaded.

I backed away, stumbling up the steps, unable to find the handrail on the wall, only damp stone. I emerged through the trapdoor into daylight. Earth strewn with straw and muck covered the castle courtyard and had replaced the expanse of grass where the knights had been fighting. The air was filled with new smells of woodsmoke and horses. Grey clouds shadowed the castle turrets. Even the castle had changed. The main building, where the state rooms were, looked as if it had shrunk and it was plainer than before, made of the same stone as the towers on either side of the gatehouse.

I hovered by the side of Caesar's Tower unsure what to do, aware of my heart thudding against my chest. The castle had been quiet with just our class and a few other visitors wandering around. But now there were people everywhere. Soldiers were gathered on the opposite side of the castle dressed in red tunics and padded jackets with a red and white coat of arms stitched into the material. Standing in line they clasped long bows and shot arrows towards targets on the castle wall. Two huge horses, covered in the same red material, snorted as they were led across the muddy yard. The clunk of metal on metal was loud from where I stood.

The glow of a fire lit up the inside of a building behind me. A boy in a dirty tunic appeared in the doorway, his arms loaded with rusty armour. His face was red, his lip curled with a scar. I turned away.

Nothing was familiar.

No signposts.

No class led by an overly enthusiastic Miss Chard.

No Danny.

Just Lizzie. She was crouched in the corner by the gatehouse where the tented entrance to the dungeon had been but only a solid stone wall now remained.

I ran across the muddy courtyard, dodging the really wet bits, past a makeshift workshop leaning against one of the outer walls. It smelt of fresh sawdust, mingled with the stronger farmyard smell outside. Everywhere I looked people were busy, feeding pigs, cleaning armour, practising with swords, preparing for something.

I reached Lizzie and she glanced up. "There's horse muck all over the place."

I knelt beside her. Her white trainers were now stained brown. Her hands shook as she ripped apart a piece of straw.

"Have you seen anyone else?" I asked.

"No." She stared past me towards the archers. "Whoever's idea of a joke this is, it's not funny."

"I don't think this is..."

"Oh just shut up, Maisie."

There were shouts from the other side of the gatehouse and then the sound of wood scraping against stone. A horse and rider galloped into the castle.

"Maybe everyone's back at the coach," I said.

"Don't you think I thought of that," she said, scrambling to her feet and towering over me. "The gate was closed before." She disappeared around the side of the gatehouse.

I got to my feet. My long dress trailed in the mud. I heard the wooden gates scraping closed. Lizzie stood just around the corner in front of the gatehouse keeper. It took two men to lift a huge piece of wood across the gates, barring them shut. The gatehouse keeper leant on a long spiked club and stared at us, his lips twitching beneath his grey beard. I didn't fancy asking him to open it up again.

I left Lizzie staring stupidly at him and darted back around the corner. The rider was over the far side of the courtyard now, shouting at the archers. I couldn't make out what he said but I knew something big was happening. I found the entrance to the barbican and started to climb the narrow stone steps. It was dark on the spiral stairway with only occasional shafts of light creeping through from the slits in the stone walls. I climbed two flights of stairs before I heard gruff, unfriendly voices. Candlelight flickered on to the steps just above me. I tiptoed past the lookout tower, hardly daring to breathe. Three bearded men sat round a wooden table, drinking. One of them looked a bit like my dad before Mum made him shave off his beard. Luckily they were too busy arguing to notice me. One of them thumped the table with his fist. I ran to the top of the steps as fast as I could and pushed the door open. I was high up, not quite as high as we'd been on Guy's Tower but I knew I'd be able to see along the path towards the rose garden and the entrance to the castle. I leant over the parapet and couldn't believe what I saw.

Chapter Two

Muddy lanes had replaced roads. Terraced houses with red roofs were now stone cottages that looked like the miniature houses from my brother Ollie's old train set. The church, pylons and cars had gone. The whole town had gone. Instead a green and brown landscape spread for miles, dotted with trees and cottages where Warwick had been. I wanted to pinch myself awake but I wasn't dreaming. I leant over the stone parapet as far as I dared. My eyes followed the dirt path out of the castle, hoping to see the school coach parked where we'd left it. I knew it wouldn't be there.

I found Lizzie hunched against the wall at the bottom of the barbican steps. She traced something in the dirt with her fingers.

"There's nothing out there."

She raised her hand. "Don't talk to me."

I bit my lip and turned away from her. I'd rather be on my own than with Lizzie. It was much louder down on the ground with the clang of metal and the whoosh of arrows. Men in uniform were busy practising with swords; a woman in a brown dress paced across the courtyard carrying bright red and yellow material towards the soldiers on the far side of the castle.

"Have you seen the time?" Lizzie asked. She stood up and brushed the dirt off her long black skirt.

I showed her my bare wrists. "I'm not wearing a watch. I didn't think it would go with a medieval costume."

She glared at me and scraped her trainer through the number four she'd written in the dirt. "It's only 2 o'clock. We've got two hours before we've got to meet back at the coach."

I frowned. "But there is no coach."

"I'm going to go search the castle for everyone," she said.

"No one's here, Lizzie. Everything's gone." I pointed to the castle entrance. "It's all changed out there. Go see for yourself."

"What are you saying?" Her pale face flushed the colour of beetroot. She stepped towards me. "That we've gone back in time?" she said and burst into tears. "Do you know how crazy you sound?"

"I never said that," I said quietly. "You said it."

She slumped back down on the ground, her body shaking with sobs. "It doesn't... make... sense..." she said, trying to catch her breath through tears. Gripping her knees so hard her knuckles and fingernails turned white, she let out a low sob.

I glanced behind me. "Shush, Lizzie, people are watching." I reached my hand out to touch her arm but she flinched away from me.

"I don't care if anyone's watching!" She curled herself tighter into a ball and started rocking. "I just want to go home."

"I want to be home too," I said, fighting back tears. Lizzie was scaring me now. "I know it sounds crazy but I feel like I've been here before."

"Of course we've been here before. It's Warwick Castle." She wiped her tears away with the back of her hand and scrambled to her feet.

"No, I mean been here, now, whenever this is." I motioned around us. "The smells, the view from up on the tower, it's all familiar, like I've seen it before."

"Girls!" An authoritative voice bellowed behind us. For a moment it sounded like Miss Chard about to tell us off for getting lost. I so wanted the voice to belong to her; I didn't care if she was angry. The grey haired, red-faced woman wasn't Miss Chard, but she was mad. With her hands on her hips she stormed over to us. "Are you the girls from the village to help with the feast tonight?"

There was a gap where one of her front teeth should have been, the rest of them were the colour of Lizzie's muddied trainers. I opened my mouth to speak but she cut me off. "You're late."

"We've lost our class," Lizzie said, still sobbing.

The woman stepped forward and clipped her round the ear. "Don't you answer me back." Lizzie flinched and her hand flew out in retaliation but the woman was quick and grabbed her arm and twisted it. "And stop your snivelling." She gripped my wrist tightly and marched us towards the castle. She smelt like wet dog.

It was dark inside, with the stone corridor lit only by smoking torches. An overpowering smell of spices got stronger the further the woman took us. I jogged to keep up with her. We reached a large, low room choked with smoke. Two log fires on either side of the room crackled and spat. Most of the smoke escaped back into the kitchen area. A boy, younger than me, sat hunched at the side of the hearth turning a whole pig on a spit. His face was smeared black with soot. Loads of people were busying about, heaving sacks across the kitchen or straining as they lifted heavy pans on to hooks above the fire.

The woman with the bad teeth pushed me towards the large wooden table in the centre of the room. "You work here," she said, letting go of me before shoving Lizzie further into the smoky room.

On the table in front of me was a wooden slab. I didn't recognise what was on it as meat to begin with as it was the colour of cooked liver, not bright red like the beef Mum bought from the butcher. The people surrounding me shouted at each other over the hiss of the flames and the clang of pans. A skinny girl stood opposite me mixing something sticky in a bowl.

"Best not stand there doing nothing," she said, nodding towards the meat in front of me.

I glanced away from her, desperate to see where Lizzie had gone.

"You a mute? That why you standing there dumb?" the skinny girl continued. "See the bowl next to you," she pointed a sticky finger at it. "Rub that into the meat."

I picked up the bowl and sniffed. I could smell cinnamon and pepper. The girl continued to stare so I put my hands into the bowl and mixed the spices with my fingers. The skinny girl looked at me through sunken eye sockets. Her skin was yellowy and her dress hung so limply off her bony frame it was difficult to tell if she was my age or older.

I caught her eye again. "What's going on?"

"You *can* speak, then," she said and grinned. "Earl of Warwick's ordered a feast tonight before setting off to battle tomorrow."

Battle? What battle? Where was Danny? And the others? They must have missed us by now. They would search the whole castle if we didn't show up at the coach. But we weren't lost – well not exactly. I knew where I was but everything was different. The smoke tickled my throat. I coughed. There was no fresh air in here or windows. It was below ground like the dungeon. I took a deep breath and started rubbing the spices into the meat. It felt dry and gritty like a piece of bark. What had happened on the dungeon steps? I'd felt the stones in the wall shift against my back and the ground had become unsteady – how I imagined an earthquake would feel. Why was Lizzie still here when no one else was? Just my luck. I tried my hardest at school to avoid her and now I was stuck with her. I caught sight of her at the far end of the room scowling as bad tooth woman showed her a sack of carrots.

"Where you from?" the skinny girl asked.

The fire behind me pumped heat into the room. I wiped the sweat dripping down the side of my face with the back of my hand. "Hay-on-Wye."

"Never heard of it."

"It's on the Welsh border, about two hours away."

"They brought you all that way and they couldn't give our Anne work tonight." She frowned and spat on the floor. I looked away from her and caught Lizzie's eye. She mouthed something.

"Two of you, eh?" the skinny girl said.

"This is all a mistake," I said. "We're not meant to be here."

"Too right you're not..."

There was a scream from the fireplace opposite me. The skinny girl leapt out of the way as the pot hanging over the fire fell on to the floor with a clang. Steaming water flooded from it, soaking into the straw. The girl in front of the fire sobbed and hopped about revealing a bright red scald on her ankle.

The woman with bad teeth stormed over and slapped the girl across the face. Her sobs stopped immediately. "You pick that up and refill it with water or you're no longer any use to me."

"I'm sorry, Mistress Baker," the girl said and dropped to the floor to heave the pot up.

I'd stopped working. Big mistake. Mistress Baker spotted me and pointed. "You," she called across the table, "come with me."

I nodded, but before following her, there was something I needed to know. I turned to the skinny girl. "What year is it?"

She frowned at me. "So, you may not be dumb but you are stupid. It's 1471 of course."

Chapter Three

1471. It was true then. We'd actually travelled back in time. It was impossible. It *had* to be impossible but somehow it felt right, like I was meant to be here. My stomach churned but from nervous excitement rather than fear. Mistress Baker clicked her fingers at me and with a deep breath I followed her down a rabbit warren of flame-lit passageways and up a flight of stone steps. The further we went, the louder the sound of voices and laughter became, and pipe music too, similar to what Miss Chard had played during our last history lesson. The Great Hall was so different from the empty hall we'd looked around a couple of hours before. Tables stretched along the length of the hall forming a ∏-shape with the head table raised on a platform. And it was full of people, mostly men and soldiers, but there were some women.

Mistress Baker handed me a jug of dark liquid. I'd had a sip of Mum's red wine once but this stuff smelt like vinegar.

"Keep their glasses full, keep 'em happy," she said, nudging me in the direction of the nearest table.

I faltered, not knowing what to do, not wanting to move. The hot smoky kitchen was better than this.

"What're you waiting for?" Mistress Baker

shouted at me.

The jug was filled to the top and heavy so I walked carefully towards the nearest table, dodging out of the way of a grey wiry dog padding across the flagstone floor. Everyone ignored me as I leant over the table and poured wine into their glasses. I counted a roast chicken to every four people. There were big earthenware pots filled with a steaming stew of meat and vegetables alongside custard-style sweets. The soldiers ate hungrily, dipping chunks of white bread into the stew sauce and taking great gulps of wine. They drank the wine almost as quickly as I filled their glasses. The head table had a roast turkey placed at its centre, behind which sat the most important-looking man in the room, who wore ruby red clothes embroidered with gold thread. I presumed the woman next to him was his wife. Her skin was so pale she looked ill and her gold-coloured dress sparkled with jewellery.

I walked back and forth with jugs of wine for hours. I lost count of how many times I filled up everyone's glasses. The banquet hall got noisier, hotter and smokier. The more wine the soldiers drank, the louder they talked and laughed until they were shouting and drowning out the music. Servants brought food in from the kitchen all night. There was a roar when two men carried in the roasted pig, still on its spit, its skin blackened and crackled. The dog whined as the pig was torn apart, its steaming flesh piled on to platters and taken to the tables by the serving girls. Lizzie must still have been stuck in the kitchen because I couldn't see her anywhere.

Towards the end of the evening the important-looking man stood up to a fanfare of trumpets and everyone fell silent. I stayed in the shadows at the edge of the hall and watched as he raised his cup.

"We leave at dawn tomorrow to join the Earl of Warwick and his army!" he roared. The soldiers leapt to their feet and with their cups raised high, yelled along with him. "To Warwick and England!"

I knew I recognised the year 1471. The man he was talking about, the Earl of Warwick, was the Kingmaker and we were in the middle of the Wars of the Roses. A few hours ago I was reading about him in my Warwick Castle booklet and now one of his men was in front of me getting his soldiers fired up for battle.

"More wine!" someone shouted and I started to work my way around the table again. Mixed with the food was the smell of people and some of them smelt bad. Lizzie always made fun of Adam Rickett's BO. I didn't think it was actually him that smelt but the hooded top he wore every single day to school. I'm sure it'd never been washed. I always felt sorry for Adam because I knew what it was like to be on the receiving end of Lizzie's bitchiness. The men smelt of sweat and their breath of stale wine. The women looked incredible in long dresses of ruby, silver and green with their hair braided beneath elaborate headdresses but I noticed, when filling up their glasses with wine, that their smiles weren't pop-star white. Not as rotten as Mistress Baker's but they'd never be able to advertise Colgate.

My head hurt from the smoke and noise and my arms ached from heaving jugs of wine around all night. I decided I never wanted to be a waitress. Or work in a kitchen. Ever. The only thing that had come close to feeling this tired was a sponsored twelve-mile walk I did over the Brecon Beacons when I was ten. But at least then I had Dad to meet me at the end, a hot bath when I got home, Mum's lasagne for dinner and my bed. Now the smell from the roasted meats made my stomach rumble. It was so long since I ate my cheese and pickle sandwich with Danny on the castle wall.

Once the flow of food stopped, the Great Hall began to empty. When there were no more glasses to fill up with wine I followed one of the other serving girls back along the narrow passageways to the kitchen. It was dark with the fireplaces barely glowing with charred embers. Lizzie crouched next to one with her arms curled round her legs. She looked as if she was asleep. The girl I'd followed joined the other kitchen girls and I was left standing alone. I wandered over to Lizzie. She didn't look up so I tapped my shoe against her trainer. "Lizzie?"

She wiped furiously at her eyes but I could tell she'd been crying. "What?"

Her fingers were red raw from scraping all those vegetables. "Are you okay?" I knew it was a lame thing to say when she obviously wasn't okay but it was all I could think of.

"Do I look okay?" she hissed. Fresh tears trickled down her pale cheeks and her shoulders shook as she hugged her knees tighter. "It's all so messed up."

A door banged and Mistress Baker stormed in. "If you want a bed for the night, follow me," she said.

I waited while Lizzie scrambled to her feet and with the rest of the kitchen staff we followed Mistress Baker across the castle courtyard. I had no idea what time it was but I could hardly keep my eyes open and figured it was stupidly late. The moon lit our way past the stables. The room she took us to was dark apart from a sliver of moonlight casting a white glow on to a stone floor covered with straw. My legs nearly buckled; I was so desperate for somewhere to lie down. I'd been hoping for the impossible: my room and my bed with my favourite Japanese print duvet cover on it.

"No way am I sleeping in here," Lizzie said, shaking her head and staggering back towards the door.

Mistress Baker moved swiftly towards Lizzie with her hand held out ready to strike her. "You're welcome to spend the night outside the castle walls if you don't mind getting robbed or worse."

I grabbed Lizzie's sleeve and pulled her to the furthest end of the room. I slumped on the floor and Lizzie huffed loudly but joined me.

"Believe it or not, straw's quite comfortable to sleep on," I said.

"What, you often sleep out in your dad's cowshed do you?"

"Hayshed actually." I scraped some straw into a pillow shape and lay down. I could feel the ground, cold and hard through the straw. It wasn't comfortable like the bales of hay me and Ollie turned into makeshift beds during the summer. Lizzie wouldn't understand the adventure of sleeping outside at night or having a midnight feast in the moonlight with Ollie and our cousins. But I was that tired I didn't care any longer what she thought or whether she managed to sleep.

~

I woke up shivering. An old man on the far side of the room coughed and spluttered. I wriggled about in the scratchy straw trying to get comfortable but it was difficult wedged between the wall and Lizzie. I could tell she was asleep because there was a slight snore at the end of every breath. I wanted to be in my bed at home with the duvet pulled up to my chin. I wanted to see moonlight through the curtains and know that Ollie was in the next room and Mum and Dad were across the hall. But I wasn't – despite all the people in the room, I was alone. Lizzie didn't count because she was no comfort. I was tempted to climb over her and escape outside and see if there was anything I recognised. But the room was too full of people sleeping where they could.

The smell was intense – BO and cheesy feet and wee. I was quite glad of the stench of smoke still up my nose. It was dark. I had no idea what time it was. I lay back down and shuffled closer to the wall.

~

"Maisie, wake up." Lizzie's voice was urgent. She shook me. I opened my eyes and flinched at the sight of her towering above me. "Everyone's leaving."

I sat up and peered around. Lizzie was even paler than normal. Mascara was smudged beneath her eyes. Her usually straight, perfectly shiny hair was lank against her shoulders. My neck was stiff and my shoulders ached. I was also dying for a wee.

"We have to go," she said, running her fingers through her hair. If Lizzie looked a mess I was so glad there wasn't a mirror to see how mad my dark curly hair was.

I struggled to my feet and shook off the straw and dirt that was stuck to my dress and tunic top. Lizzie paced in front of me. There were only a few people left in the room including the old man who'd been coughing his guts up all night. Typical – he was asleep now. At least, I presumed he was asleep...

"Come on," Lizzie said, and pulled me towards the wooden door at the end of the room.

The sun had risen but it couldn't be much past dawn and goosebumps covered my arms. The castle courtyard was filled with horses, carts, boys and soldiers busy cleaning their swords, heaving sacks on to wagons and grooming their horses. The castle gates were still closed. A few of the people we'd shared the room with last night hovered by the gatehouse, ready to be let out of the castle and into Warwick.

Lizzie and me waited in the sunshine in silence. Mistress Baker was nowhere to be seen and I wasn't sure what we were supposed to do now. I wanted someone to tell me what to do. Lizzie frowned and bit her nails. I took a couple of steps away from her and watched the soldiers gathering on the other side of the courtyard. I recognised a couple of them from the feast. There was a boy wearing the same uniform as the soldiers but his hair was shaved at the sides and spiky on top. I strained to see him properly, and then he half-turned towards me.

"Danny!"

Chapter Four

There were footsteps behind me and Lizzie clamped her hand over my mouth. She pulled me back into the shadow of Caesar's Tower. "Are you crazy?"

I struggled away from her grip and turned on her. "Danny's with the soldiers."

"I don't care who's with them. You're going to get us in trouble screaming like that."

"You didn't care when you were having a full-on hissy fit yesterday," I said, pushing her away. "You don't get it, do you? Danny's here, with us." There was a bang and a crunch as the castle gates scraped open. "I'm going after him, I'm following the soldiers." I started walking towards the gate but stopped when Lizzie didn't follow me. "What's the point in staying here?"

"How do you think anyone's going to find us if we leave?" she said, her voice rising like she was going to burst into tears again.

"You really think we're going to be found? It's the fifteenth century. We're not born for another five hundred years."

Lizzie shook her head and backed away from me. She kicked at the ground before leaning against the castle wall with her head in her hands. I glanced towards the soldiers. Danny had been swallowed up by the mass of flags, swords and axes that the men were loading on to carts.

"How are you so sure that following them is the right thing to do?" Lizzie asked.

"I'm not. I've just got this strong feeling that it's what we're meant to do. Anyway, if it was you with the soldiers instead of Danny, wouldn't you want us to come after you?"

"Okay fine," she finally said. "We'll go with them. But just wait a minute."

Before I could say anything, she'd run off towards the servants' quarters and kitchen. The armoured horses closest to the castle gates pounded the ground with their hooves, as impatient as I was to get going. Danny had disappeared but there might be others from our class caught up with the soldiers. We couldn't hang about the castle forever. I shivered. It was early enough for dew to still be clinging to the grass. I was so glad Mum had made me a long-sleeved tunic to go under her old oversized grey dress and had forced me to wear thick tights. I had an old pair of ankle boots on that we'd dyed a muddy brown colour – they looked sort of authentic.

With a clang of armour the first rider thundered out of the castle gates and the others followed, the wheels of loaded carts creaking as they turned. I glanced in the direction that Lizzie had disappeared and wondered what she was doing. How long should I wait for her? The skinny girl from the kitchen stood by the gatehouse cheering the soldiers on. I didn't particularly like her but I'd rather be standing over there with her than waiting on my own. Anyway, I'd have more of a chance of seeing Danny if I was closer.

The skinny girl was too busy watching the army file past to notice me. The clang of armour was deafening and there was a strong smell of leather and sweaty men and horses. One of the carts rolled past and the girl and her friends ran alongside it, waving until they disappeared through the gatehouse. I was on my own again. Danny had definitely been up towards the front of the Kingmaker's army so he'd probably left the castle by now. Why was I waiting for Lizzie? She wouldn't do the same for me.

I was about to move when someone flicked the back of my head. "Let's go." Lizzie walked past me with something bundled in her arms.

"I was about to go without you."

"Like I'd care."

"I see you're back to your usual self then." I should have left her and gone off with the skinny girl and her friends. Anyone was better than Lizzie.

"You should be thanking me. I got food," she said. "For our journey." She unfolded a piece of cloth to reveal a chunk of bread and cold cooked meat. "There's loads left from last night."

"Lucky you didn't get caught."

"You'd have loved that, wouldn't you?"

"Do you not remember the torture chamber?" I said, striding past her.

I half-expected us to walk through the gatehouse and find ourselves back in the present, or as it would be now, the future. We didn't.

The view I'd seen yesterday from the top of the castle lay before us unchanged. Outside the castle walls, Warwick was little more than a village. The kitchen girls headed down the dirt path towards a cluster of cottages. Home for us was two hours in the other direction by coach. *By coach.* How long would it take to walk – days and days – and what would we find when we got there? But the Kingmaker's army was marching in the opposite direction, past Warwick and away from our home, their armour glinting in the early morning sunshine. In every direction there was an uncluttered landscape filled with green grass and trees. No pylons, no roads, no landmarks or signposts. I stopped just a few steps from the castle gates where the path to the car park had been.

"This is a stupid idea," Lizzie said, stopping beside me.

"Have you got a better one? Like go back inside and wait to be rescued?"

"Fine." She glared at me and scuffed at the dirt with her ruined Nikes. "What are we waiting for then?"

"I'm just trying to figure out where they're marching."

"To battle."

"Yes, but which one?"

"What does it matter?"

"What if we lose them?"

"You're kidding, right? There are hundreds of

them."

"I know that, but they're going to march to battle quicker than we're going to be able to walk and keep up with them." I set off again down the sloping dirt path that followed the length of the castle walls to the river, not really caring if Lizzie followed or not. The grey walls of the castle dominated the skyline. They looked solid and protective but we were on the wrong side. I tried to think back to being in the castle when everything was normal. I tried to remember what I'd read in the castle brochure and in the rooms as we walked around. And at school. Miss Chard had spent ages talking to us about the Wars of the Roses. When we'd walked through the waxwork exhibition in the castle we'd listened to the Kingmaker's speech before battle. Richard Neville, the Earl of Warwick, had swapped sides and wanted to keep Edward IV off the throne. So this meant we were following Neville – the Kingmaker's army – to the battle of... "Barnet."

"What?" Lizzie snapped from a couple of steps behind me.

"It's the Battle of Barnet we're going to. And if we're following the Earl of Warwick's army it means Danny's with the losing side." I walked faster, desperate now to find him and get him out of danger.

Lizzie and I didn't talk. This was typical behaviour for her. When she wasn't having a go at me at school she would ignore me. The only sound was the rhythmic thud, thud, thud of the soldiers and the occasional neigh of a horse. Holding the bundle of food in one hand, Lizzie reached into her skirt pocket and pulled out her pink iPod and earphones and plugged herself in. The tinny sound of One Direction through her earphones sounded odd considering the circumstances.

We left the castle walls behind and began walking alongside the river. We were still wearing the clothes we'd changed into when we first got to Warwick Castle and hadn't washed in over twenty-four hours. I wanted to stop and drink from the river and splash my face with water but we couldn't lose the army. Without a map or signposts we'd never make it to Barnet. I guess we could always ask someone, although the skinny girl looked blank when I'd mentioned Hay-on-Wye. I glanced at Lizzie. She didn't seem to be looking at or thinking about anything. She clutched the food parcel to her like a comfort blanket.

I pretended it was the summer holidays and I was on a walk in the Forest of Dean and it was my brother Ollie next to me listening to the The Script on his iPod rather than Lizzie giving off "get away from me" vibes. The path continued to follow the winding river and it gave me something to look at besides the army marching ahead. The village had disappeared behind a hill and the children waving and shouting after the army had wandered off. I glanced back at the impressive outline of Warwick Castle, the only thing disturbing the skyline. I didn't want to lose sight of it or feel as though I'd lost our only connection to home. If Ollie was here he'd say something to make me feel better, to reassure me I was doing the right thing walking towards the unknown. They'd be so worried at home. How would school have explained our disappearance? What if we never got back? I shivered and concentrated instead on the river and the trees lining the opposite bank. Pale green buds had sprouted on the branches and pink blossom was the only other colour in the landscape besides the army. I couldn't help but feel a tiny bit excited, after all, this was the stuff of films, being able to travel back in time and see the reality behind the history books. But this was way better than a film. This was real.

Chapter Five

We stopped when the army stopped. The sun was now high in the sky and I sweated from the pace the army set. We'd pretty much followed the river the whole time, only veering off when the way forward got too muddy or completely impassable. Lizzie plonked herself on a rock at the edge of the river and I sat opposite her. She unwrapped the food and waved it in my direction.

"Do you want some?" she asked.

"Yes please." I reached forward and took a piece of dry bread and a chunk of meat. Lizzie popped a piece of bread into her mouth and we chewed in silence for a while. All I could think about was Mum's lasagne and sweet and sour chicken with egg fried rice from the Chinese.

"I wish this was a double cheeseburger and we were in McDonald's instead of here," Lizzie said and spat a chewed lump of bread on to the grass and ripped off a piece of meat instead. "That bread was off yesterday."

I slid off the rock and crouched down. "Wash the bread down with water," I said. I cupped my hands together and dipped them in the river. The water was icy cold and tasted better than bottled water – actually it tasted better than a cold bottle of Coke right that minute.

"Yuck," Lizzie said, scrunching up her face.

I dipped my hands in again, gulped down some more freezing water and washed my face. "What's the problem?" I asked.

"You've no idea what's in that water."

"Lizzie, the water is perfectly safe, much safer than what comes out of your tap at home."

"I like what comes out of the tap."

For all the confident know-it-all front she put on at school, she was pathetic. I never spent any time outside of school with Lizzie. If I caught sight of her in town with her friends I'd walk the other way. I wasn't particularly enjoying getting to know her. I turned my back on her and dipped my hands in the river again. It took a lot of effort to get a decent drink of water.

"Maisie."

I trailed my fingers in the water and watched a pink blossom float past.

"Maisie." Her tone was urgent and half-whispered.

"What?"

When she didn't reply I glanced behind me. Less than ten paces away was a seriously large dog. It was smaller than Benji, our Great Dane, but looked fifty times as mean. Saliva dribbled from its snarling jaws. It growled at Lizzie.

"Don't move," I said.

"Really?" she hissed back at me.

I needed to move though; my legs were beginning to ache from crouching by the edge of the river. "Is there any meat left?"

"Uh, huh."

"Chuck it some."

Something thudded on the ground. The dog's growl grew more intense. My knees were hurting so badly now. I slowly pulled myself up until I was standing and turned around. The dog's black eyes switched from Lizzie to me.

"It's interested in us, not the food," Lizzie said.

"That's because we are the food."

"Oh shut up, Maisie."

"We could run in opposite directions and confuse it," I said.

A blast of a horn sounded and the dog's head shot up.

"Run now!" I shouted. I legged it along the grassy path next to the river, hoping Lizzie had the sense to follow me and she wasn't being mauled... I concentrated on forcing my legs to move faster. There was a howl from the direction I'd run from.

"Maisie!" So she hadn't been eaten. "Maisie!"

I turned back. Lizzie wasn't far behind but the dog had disappeared. I slowed to a jog and stopped when she reached me.

"It's lame," she said between panting. "I'm not going any further." She folded her arms and her bottom lip jutted out as if she was about to cry. "I'm going back to Warwick."

"What good will going back do? It was just a dog."

"You didn't know it was lame. It could have killed us."

"But it didn't." I wiped my damp hands on my

dress and continued to walk along the well-trodden path the soldiers were following. "Think of it as an adventure," I called over my shoulder.

We skirted the wood and followed the curve of the river. The rumble of soldiers' voices, the snort of horses and crunch of armour gradually grew louder. I stopped the moment the soldiers were in sight. Not only was the army we'd followed from Warwick spread out along the riverbank but another army three or four times the size was marching in from the opposite direction.

"How are we going to find Danny now?" Lizzie asked.

"I have no idea." There were now thousands of soldiers in front of us. It would be like looking for a blade of grass in a cornfield.

"You still want to follow them?"

"What else can we do?"

Lizzie, with her hands on her hips, gaped at the army and shook her head. "This is total madness." She glared at me.

"Why are you blaming me?" My palms felt sweaty. What started as an adventure was getting scary. Coming across that wild dog had reminded me this wasn't a game. It had scared Lizzie more but I was worried about what else we would meet. Plus we'd already eaten most of our food and left a piece of meat lying in the grass for that dog. If we left the river we had nothing to carry drinking water in. A few more hours and it would get dark and we were two twelve-year-old girls stuck in the fifteenth century. Mum and Dad let me stay out late on our farm in the summer but in the winter I had to be in before dark. They'd be going crazy at the moment wondering where I was and how I would cope with another night alone.

Lizzie sat down in the long grass and started to make a necklace from the strands of grass surrounding us. I watched the soldiers. At the front of the larger army were flag bearers and soldiers on horseback next to an important-looking man on a beautiful grey stallion. He commanded all the attention from the soldiers and I presumed he was the Earl of Warwick. I remembered from our history lesson that he'd be dead by the end of the Battle of Barnet. Trumpets played a fanfare and then Warwick greeted the leader of the army we'd been following. I recognised him as the man who'd made the speech at the banquet the night before.

"Isn't Barnet near London?" Lizzie asked, not looking up from her grass necklace.

"I think so."

"Do you realise how far away from Warwick that is?"

"A few days' walk maybe."

"You're joking, right? Where are we supposed to sleep? What are we going to eat?"

"We'll sort something out," I said.

"This isn't one of your slumming it camping holidays."

"What's that supposed to mean?"

She shook her head and chucked her grass necklace away. "I mean we could *die* out here."

She practically whispered the word "die" as if saying it out loud would make it happen.

"We're not going to die. We can survive for a few days and nights on our own. Have you never watched Bear Grylls?"

"Who?"

"He's an explorer who goes all over the world and survives in remote places where there's no food or water."

"What? Like in *I'm a Celebrity, Get Me Out of Here*?"

"It's nothing like *I'm a Celeb*."

"Good because I'm not eating bugs."

I gave up; she didn't get it. She was the worst person to be stuck here with. I turned back to the army. The soldiers furthest away from us, led by Warwick, were beginning to march off and there was a lot of movement in the rest of the ranks. The army was so big now the soldiers at the front would be miles ahead of us by the time everyone got moving.

"We're going to Portugal for Easter," Lizzie said. "My parents have got a villa overlooking the beach there. Have you ever been to Portugal?"

I shook my head. "We don't really go away much because of the farm."

"That sucks."

"Not really, I don't mind."

I expected that attitude from Lizzie with her family's four-storey townhouse, holidays abroad at least twice a year and a Mum who dropped her at the school gates in a brand new Range Rover. Dad would only drive Ollie and me to school when it rained and then I'd have to sit on a bale of straw in the back of our battered Land Rover.

"What did you mean when you said yesterday in the castle that it felt like you've been here before?" Lizzie asked.

"Just that, it's all familiar, like I've got permanent déjà vu."

"Even now?"

I nodded. "I feel like we're meant to be here."

"If you say so. Explains why you're way too calm and being a complete freak enjoying all of this."

Finally the soldiers nearest us were on the move. I stood up and brushed off the dried grass and soil stuck to my dress. I waited while Lizzie sighed loudly and scrambled to her feet. She stuffed the cloth with the rest of the bread into her pocket and shoved her iPod earphones back in. I wondered how long it would be until the battery ran out.

Chapter Six

Every part of me ached. My legs felt heavy as if I'd been dragging them through sand all day. Lizzie had remained silent the whole time, even after her iPod stopped working. I hadn't had the energy to feel even a little bit smug. We lagged behind. At times we lost sight of the army altogether but we could still hear their rhythmic thud, thud, thud and clang of armour in the distance. The trail of flattened grass from hundreds of footprints was easy to follow.

The army stopped when the light began to fade. To our right was the river and to the left a gloomy wood.

"It looks like we're staying here for the night," I said.

"Great, looks real cosy."

The army had blankets and makeshift tents on the carts. We had... Well we had nothing. We needed water, shelter, warmth and food. The river sorted the water problem – Lizzie had been forced to drink straight from the river after going nearly all day without any. As for shelter... I headed for the wood.

Lizzie ran to catch up with me. "No way am I sleeping in there."

"Where else do you suggest?" I looked back at the expanse of grass sloping towards the river. "I don't fancy sleeping out in the open." I plucked a leafy frond from a large fern. "Let's find loads of leaves like this to use as bedding."

Lizzie's mouth dropped open as if she was about to argue with me. Instead she stomped off to gather leaves.

It was dark and raining by the time we'd padded the ground beneath the largest tree at the edge of the wood. I wanted to be sheltered from the rain but any further into the wood was way too scary. I liked being able to see the river and the orange glow of the army's fires.

"We can always rub two sticks together," I said, barely having the energy to talk, let alone "make fire". Lizzie just grunted.

I closed my eyes and imagined I was in a tent. The sound of the rain falling on the leaves above was similar to rain drumming on canvas and the tree was keeping us surprisingly dry. But my grumbling stomach kept me awake. I'd never been so hungry. All I could think about was roast beef and Yorkshire puddings, apple pie and custard, even ham and pickle sandwiches, anything to fill my empty stomach. Despite Lizzie's moaning about sleeping outside she was already snoring.

This was our second night away from home but it felt so much longer than that. Even though I was more tired than I'd ever felt before I didn't think I could get to sleep. I thought about being at home on our farm and the chores and homework I'd be doing before sitting down for dinner with Mum, Dad and Ollie. I snuggled down into my makeshift bed of leaves and tucked some spare fronds over the top of me in an attempt to stay warm.

~

I couldn't open my eyes. I stretched my legs and felt pain in every muscle. I forced my eyes open. I was half-sitting, half-lying against the tree trunk. The view was like opening a tent flap on the most beautiful desolate place. The river sparkled in the sunshine and the grass spreading in front of us was a vivid green. Lizzie was curled in a ball next to me with her eyes closed.

I struggled to sit up. "Are you awake?" She curled her arms tighter around herself and shook her head. I sighed. "I'm just going down to the river."

Walking through the long wet grass I worked the ache out of my legs and shoulders. The sun felt very warm for us having just woken up but I had no idea what time it was. I squatted at the edge of the river and took great gulps of water before washing my face and neck. I wanted to go for a swim but the water was freezing plus I only had the clothes I was wearing and I didn't fancy skinny-dipping. I stood up, closed my eyes and leant my head back to let my face dry in the sun. I could only hear birds singing and the slap of the river flowing over rocks but no voices. It was too quiet. My heart thudded in my chest. I jogged along the edge of the river and rounded the corner. Last night's fires were charred wood and ash and the only things left to show the army had been there were discarded meat bones and large piles of droppings from the horses. How long had we slept for? How had we not heard the army marching off?

I raced back to the tree. Lizzie was propped up against the trunk, scowling.

"They've gone," I said.

"What?"

"The army has already left."

Lizzie sneezed. "Like I care. I'm not going anywhere, I feel like rubbish."

"What do you suggest we do if we don't follow them?"

"Sleep."

I crouched next to her and put my hand against her forehead. She shrugged me off.

"You're really hot. Let's at least get to a village and see if we can get a proper bed for the night."

"Oh you've got a map have you, to miraculously find a village?" Her face got redder and redder and then she burst into tears. "Just leave me here," she sobbed. I should have enjoyed seeing her in a state but I didn't. I was worried that she really was ill.

"Don't be silly, I'm not leaving you." I had every intention of still following the army but I had to find a way to get Lizzie moving. "Anyway, we need to find some food."

Her head shot up. "Oh, I'm so hungry."

"Let's get going then."

~

Lizzie washed in the river and we shared the rest of the stale bread soaked in water so we could swallow it. Lizzie looked pale with dark shadows under her eyes. If I'd looked like that back home

Mum would have kept me off school, tucked up in bed with a hot water bottle and an endless supply of honey and lemon drinks. Each step was an effort but we had to keep going. I kept thinking of Danny with the army. Every hour that passed took him closer to the battle and further away from us.

"Let's stop for a bit," I said, when Lizzie trailed way behind me. She collapsed on the grass and put her head in her hands. I walked a bit further along the river. We were still following the army; the multiple footprints in the mud and trampled grass at least kept me positive. I had no idea how far ahead they were but I knew the distance between them and us was growing rapidly.

"Where're you going?" Lizzie called after me.

I walked back to her. "I was seeing the way ahead."

"You're loving this, aren't you?"

I shook my head. "I'm just trying to make the best of it." I certainly didn't hate it the way she did. But then Lizzie tended to hate anything she wasn't good at.

"Do you like being a tomboy?" she asked.

"I didn't know I was."

She sniffed and rubbed her eyes. "You're kidding, right? You always hang around with Danny, you never wear any make-up and do you even own a skirt?"

"Only the one my mum made me wear to my cousin's wedding."

"Point proven," she said.

Despite being sick and tired she was still

managing to be horrible. Maybe I should have left her behind. I had no interest in Lizzie and her friends. Why would I want to be anything like her, all precious over straightening her hair and painting her nails? With her blonde hair, fashionable clothes and pout she was a wannabe pop star. I liked being friends with Danny and playing football instead of going shopping. I didn't think I was missing out on anything. At least I was proving to be tougher than Lizzie Andrews.

"I'm wearing a dress now," I said.

"Ha, ha, very funny."

I ignored her. "We have to get moving again."

"Who made you boss?" she snapped. But she stood up and followed me.

The soldiers' footprints eventually led us away from the river and along a well-trodden path through a dense wood. I noticed how quiet it was with just the sound of our footsteps and the occasional twittering bird for company. Lizzie started humming to herself. I was hopeful this path would eventually lead to a town.

"Shush," I said to Lizzie. I grabbed her arm and we stopped in the middle of the path. We listened to voices and the creak of wheels, heading in our direction.

I dragged Lizzie into the undergrowth at the side of the road and we huddled behind a tree. A skinny horse appeared round the bend in the path pulling a covered wagon. The horse's mane was matted with dirt and its grey coat was stained with mud. Holding the reins at the front of the wagon was a man as dirty and skinny as the horse. A girl younger than us sat next to him. The man talked to someone inside the wagon and a woman's voice answered him. "We have to stop, I need a piss!"

"We'll never get there," the man said, scowling as he reined in the horse. It didn't take much persuading for the poor horse to stop. It dropped its head and searched the ground for grass. A woman in a brown dress eased herself down from the back of the wagon.

"If we're late we'll miss a day's pay," the man muttered. The girl next to him nodded. The woman disappeared behind the wagon.

"Are they, like, gypsies?" Lizzie whispered.

I shrugged. They looked like they had a hard life whoever they were. I wondered where they were heading and what they were going to be late for.

"Let's ask them where the nearest town is," Lizzie said, and before I could stop her she'd stepped out from the cover of the tree.

Chapter Seven

The little girl noticed Lizzie first and tugged the sleeve of the man next to her. Lizzie stopped right in front of them.

"What we got here, then?" the man said, peering down at her.

"Hi," she said. "My name's Elizabeth Andrews. We're kind of lost and wondered if you know where the nearest town is?"

"Who's we?"

"Harold?" a woman's voice called. "Who you talking to?"

"Some girl," he yelled before turning back to Lizzie. "Your friend shy?"

Lizzie glanced towards me. Great, she hadn't let me shout to Danny in the castle and she'd been terrified of the dog, but she was happy to walk right up to strangers in the middle of nowhere. I took a deep breath and stepped out from behind the tree.

"Another one," the man said.

"We're just trying to find the nearest town," I said, joining Lizzie.

The woman appeared around the side of the wagon, tugging down her skirts. She stopped in her tracks. "What do they want?"

The girl on the wagon stared down at us. I figured she was the daughter, the man and woman were her parents and that meant – I hoped – we were relatively safe despite standing like idiots in front of them.

"These girls want to know where the nearest town is."

"Well tell them and let's be on our way."

"Towcester's less than half a day's walk in that direction," he said, pointing the way we were heading. "That's where we're going if you want a ride."

His wife tutted. "They could be nothing but thieves."

The man laughed. "We ain't got nothing for them to steal." He turned back to us. "But it'll cost you."

"But if you're going there anyway," Lizzie said.

I pinched her. "That's fine, we can pay but only when we get to Towcester."

I held my breath hoping he'd agree and Lizzie would keep her mouth shut.

"Get in the back with your mother," he said to his wide-eyed daughter. The girl jumped down and Harold patted the empty space next to him. "Up you come then."

I nudged Lizzie. "After you *Elizabeth*," I said, and waited for her to move forwards. This was her idea so she could sit next to him. I clambered on to the wagon after her. It was so good to sit down even though it was on a hard wooden bench. Harold got the poor horse moving and we rolled along at a surprisingly brisk pace. Lizzie sat pressed tight against me. I could smell Harold from where I was sitting – a disgusting combination of stale sweat and something else I really hoped wasn't wee. At least we could rest our legs for a while. I was pretty sure Lizzie wouldn't have been able to walk for even another hour.

"We have no money," Lizzie whispered.

"I know but we're heading towards a town and hopefully in the same direction as the army a lot faster than if we walked."

We trundled along in silence. The trees were so dense we were continuously in the shade and I began to get goosebumps now we were sitting doing nothing. Lizzie shivered too. I pulled my sleeves down over my hands.

"Have you seen the army?" I asked.

Harold looked sharply at me. "There's talk of an army on the move. But I stay well away from that sort of thing."

"See," Lizzie hissed.

I stayed quiet and concentrated on trying to stop my stomach from rumbling. We'd find the army again; thousands of soldiers would be hard to miss. My only fear was that we'd be too late to find Danny...

~

Despite having no castle, Towcester was bigger than Warwick. I weighed up our options as we rumbled into the town along a muddy road flanked by houses. We had no money to pay Harold, let alone to buy food or a bed for the night. We could beg or steal... We passed a church set back from the town, surrounded by trees and a large graveyard. I took everything in, making a mental picture of good hiding places.

Harold reined the horse to a stop outside an inn. "Whoa there." He turned to us. "Now a penny from each of you if you please."

"Our aunt has money," I said, clambering down and motioning for Lizzie to follow. "If you give us a minute..." I waited until Lizzie's foot touched the ground. "Run!"

I legged it in the opposite direction to the way Harold and his wagon were facing. Lizzie was next to me and our legs pounded the muddy road. I didn't want to imagine what would happen to us if we were caught. With mud splattering up the backs of our legs we ran into the graveyard. We didn't stop until the church was between Harold and us.

I peered around the corner of the church. "I don't think anyone followed us."

Lizzie was bent over with her hands on her knees. "You've turned us into criminals," she said between breaths.

"We hitched a lift and didn't pay. That's not exactly stealing."

"Believe what you want," she said, standing up straight. "How are we going to get food and a bed for the night now we're fugitives?"

"Don't be so dramatic. Harold and his family will move on and we'll be forgotten about."

"And in the meantime?" she said with her hands on her hips.

"We go on the hunt for food and water." I felt

rebellious and didn't care if surviving here would go against everything that was right back home. It was 1471 after all, not the twenty-first century. I wandered among the gravestones reading the ages of the dead, which ranged from a beloved son aged three months to a positively ancient sixty-one.

"This place is freaking me out," Lizzie whispered, as if she was afraid of disturbing the dead.

"The church might be a safe place to sleep." I walked over to the door, slid the wooden bar across where it was wedged closed and gently pushed. The door creaked open. I beckoned to Lizzie and we slipped inside, closing the door behind us. It took a while for our eyes to adjust to the dusky light. Lizzie stayed close to me as we walked down the aisle between the wooden pews. I knew we had to have somewhere sheltered to sleep but it was still light and I was conscious of Danny and the army getting further and further away from us.

The door scraped open and daylight crept in. I pulled Lizzie down behind the pews at the back of the church.

"I know you're in here," Harold's voice echoed inside the church.

I held my breath and Lizzie tensed beside me. "See, bad idea," she whispered.

"Half the town saw you run this way," Harold continued. His boots thudded loudly on the flagstones. "Then I followed your muddy footprints. I only want my two pennies – a deal's a deal."

I motioned to Lizzie to follow, and crawling on our hands and knees we made our way slowly along the far wall of the church, skirting the pews. The cold flagstones bruised my knees and palms. I held my hand out to stop Lizzie when we reached the middle pews. I strained my head forward and saw Harold standing in the middle of the aisle.

"I know you're in here," he said, flicking a rope he held in one hand gently on to his other palm.

I took a deep breath and continued forward; we were nearly there, and I could see the patch of daylight on the flagstone nearest to the door... Thud. Lizzie's iPod clattered on the floor. I scooped it up, grabbed Lizzie by her sleeve and pulled her to her feet.

"You little..." Harold swung to face us as we ran the few paces to the door and slipped out of the church, slamming it shut behind us.

"Help me close it!" I said, heaving the wooden bar across. Together we wedged it shut. The full weight of Harold landed against the door but it stayed closed.

Breathless, my heart thudded against my ribs. On the other side of the churchyard was a low wall next to a gnarled old tree with a ploughed field beyond.

"Come on!" I sprinted to the wall and launched myself over, landing in soft soil on the other side. I glanced back to the church and Lizzie trailing after me. Harold was locked inside for the moment but I so didn't want to be there when he escaped. "We need to get away from here."

Lizzie nodded but despite being back out in the sunshine she was scarily pale and her teeth chattered. We tramped across the field leaving deep footprints in the soil. The field was enormous and stretched all the way to a cluster of cottages set away from Towcester. I headed for the shadow of a large oak tree near the first cottage and waited for Lizzie to catch up. She breathed heavily and was now pale and sweaty.

"Are you okay?" I asked.

"Of course."

"You're so not. If you want to rest here, I'll have a look around."

"Fine," she said and leant back against the trunk. I carefully picked my way to the edge of the field and squatted in the tall grass.

"Maisie, wait!" Lizzie hissed at me. I turned round to see her padding over. She crouched next to me. "We shouldn't split up."

The cottage nearest us was a long low building with greying whitewashed walls and a thatched roof. Two similar cottages stood further away alongside the dirt track that headed back to Towcester. I didn't fancy breaking into the cottage – we weren't that desperate yet. But there was a vegetable garden and chickens to the side of the cottage.

"Do you think you can manage to pull up some vegetables?" I asked.

"If it means we get to eat, then yes."

We crept through the long grass bordering the field, skirted the cottage and tiptoed over to the vegetable patch.

"What should I pull up?" Lizzie asked.

There wasn't much to choose from, so I showed her what looked like the tops of radishes and she started digging.

"Where are you going?" she whispered.

"To get us some eggs."

A makeshift wooden fence surrounded the chickens. I opened the rickety gate and crept in. A couple of chickens scrabbled around in the dirt but I ignored them and headed for the sheltered straw-filled corner where another six chickens were.

"Hey chickie chickies," I said, reaching my hand into the straw beneath them. They squawked and scattered as my hand closed around a smooth egg. With my other hand I lifted the front of my tunic up and dropped the egg into it before grabbing another one. The chickens squawked and flapped and one pecked my hand as I scrambled to my feet. They weren't friendly like our chickens at home.

Lizzie met me outside the pen. "Could you be any louder?"

"We have eggs," I said.

"And vegetables," she replied, holding up a big bunch of radishes.

We jogged past the cottages towards the road that would take us away from the town.

"I've never been so excited about eating radishes," Lizzie said when we reached the muddy lane and turned our backs on Towcester.

"Me neither."

Ahead of us the road disappeared into a wood. I stopped.

"What is it?" Lizzie asked.

"I have no idea what direction we're going in or if we're even following the army."

"What difference does it make? We can't exactly hang around here."

Lizzie was right – not only were we on the run from Harold but we'd stolen someone's eggs and radishes and I knew from Miss Chard's history lessons the punishment for that was being put in the stocks and pelted with rotten food. We set off for the wood again. It was the first proper road we had come across so I presumed it led to a big town, maybe even London. I felt a bit more hopeful. We could stop somewhere sheltered in the wood and try and start a fire to cook on and keep us warm. These eggs were awkward to carry in my tunic...

Clip clop, clip clop...

"Well, well, well, who do we have here?" The voice was too deep and well-spoken to belong to Harold.

We turned to see two men on horses come to a halt in front of us.

"I was warned about a couple of vagrant girls in the area," the same man said. He was dressed in riding clothes trimmed with gold thread and he looked wealthy compared to the other man. He looked us up and down and smiled. "A couple of time shifters I do believe."

I frowned. "What did you call us?"

He winked and dismounted. He strolled over and leant towards me. He smelt... nice. As if he was wearing aftershave. I wasn't expecting that.

"What year are you from?" he whispered.

I took a step back. He beckoned to us and when we were close enough to him he said, "I was born in 1980."

Chapter Eight

"1980?" Lizzie said. "I don't understand."

He grinned and I noticed his teeth were white. He was clean-shaven apart from a neatly trimmed goatee. He might be wealthy but in 1471 wealth didn't mean that someone was hygienic. He held out his hand and, still clutching the eggs in my tunic, I shook it with my free one. "I'm officially known as Robert but you can call me Robbie," he said with a wink.

Lizzie was trying to hold on to the radishes and shake Robbie's extended hand at the same time.

"I think we should go somewhere less exposed to chat. You look cold and hungry," he said, glancing at our stolen goods.

"We can take these back..." I said.

"No need," he said with a smile. "As Lord of the Manor I own all of this land anyway, so legally those radishes belong to me. Just leave them here." He pointed to the grass at the side of the road.

Lizzie chucked the radishes down and I placed the eggs next to them. He looked the part of a lord with his "doublet and hose" as Miss Chard would have said.

"My house isn't far. One of you can ride behind me," he said, patting the saddle, "and we'll get you some food and dry clothes."

"I'm not getting up on that thing," Lizzie said.

"You ride, we'll follow," I said, not really caring about walking a bit further as long as we eventually got to eat something.

Robbie launched himself on to his horse and reined her back towards Towcester.

Lizzie grabbed my arm. "That's it? We're going to go with him just like that?"

"Don't you get it? He's from the future. He could help us get back," I whispered. Robbie slowed down. We were still standing in the middle of the road where he'd found us.

"Is there a problem?" he called back.

I looked at Lizzie. "We so need new clothes, food and a proper wash."

"Fine," she said and we started walking. I hoped that if we bumped into Harold, Robbie would be protection enough. But before we reached the stone gate leading into Towcester we turned off to the right and followed the wall surrounding the town.

"This is totally insane," Lizzie whispered as we followed Robbie and his silent companion across an open field. "I mean if he's from the future then he's stuck here – we're stuck here."

"We don't know that."

"It's pretty obvious to me. He said he was born in 1980, and if he's Lord of the Manor he could have been here for years... This is a nightmare."

"I don't get it though, he seems happy."

Through the trees ahead I glimpsed the stonework of a large house. I nudged Lizzie and pointed.

"Wow," she said, "he wasn't kidding about being a lord."

The manor house disappeared from sight as we followed Robbie along a shadowy path beneath the trees. The sun was low in the sky. We hadn't eaten all day and I wanted food so badly. I shivered and was glad to feel the sunshine on my face again when we emerged through the trees and the house reappeared.

Robbie dismounted and handed the reins to his servant who led the horses to the stable block on the far side of the courtyard.

"Not bad is it?" he said, pushing open the large oak door. Inside it was dusky and smelt of woodsmoke – a really lovely smell after the castle and Harold. Robbie led us from the entrance hall into a large room that looked like a smaller version of the Great Hall in Warwick Castle. It was empty apart from a long wooden table and chairs in the centre of the hall, a huge fireplace and Coats of Arms on the walls.

"Make yourselves comfortable and I'll get cook to bring us some food."

"Robbie," I called before he reached the door. "Thank you."

"Don't mention it."

We headed for the fireplace and warmed our hands over the flames. We had a real fire in our living room at home but I'd never appreciated it as much as I did this one.

"You've got leaves and mud in your hair,"

Lizzie said.

"You don't look too great yourself." Her hair was tangled and her eyes were red and puffy.

"I guess that's what sleeping outdoors does to you... and me," she said quietly.

We both fell silent. I turned my attention back to the room. The fireplace was large enough to cook on and opened out on to a floor laid with flagstones.

"How did he end up being lord of a place like this, anyway?" I asked.

Lizzie shrugged. "I've no idea but I'm glad he is."

The door creaked open and Robbie returned, followed by a servant holding a steaming pot in her hands.

"Rabbit casserole," he said. "Sit yourselves down."

Robbie placed himself at the head of the table and me and Lizzie sat opposite each other. Another servant – better dressed than we were – entered the hall and set a plate and spoon in front of us. The first servant spooned a mound of casserole on to our plates and I tucked into warm rabbit, carrots and onion. "This is so good," I said.

"I caught and killed the rabbit myself," Robbie said and winked.

Lizzie frowned but carried on eating.

I'd only had a few mouthfuls and already I was feeling full. I wasn't going to leave a thing though – Mum would be proud.

The servants poured what looked like wine

into tumblers and then Robbie waved them away with his hand. He waited until they'd closed the door behind them before turning back to us and clasping his hands together on the table.

"Now, where were we?" he said with a grin. "I'm Robert, Lord of Towcester as I'm known here but I was born Robert O'Rourke – but always known as Robbie – in London in 1980. Now, I'd love to know who you two are."

Lizzie had a mouthful of food so I answered. "I'm Maisie Brown and this is Lizzie – Elizabeth – Andrews and we're twelve."

"I'm thirteen," Lizzie said through a mouthful of food.

"And what year have you come from?"

"2012."

Robbie whistled. "Really, that far ahead."

Lizzie frowned. "Why, how long have you been here?"

"What would seem a lifetime to you – nine years. I time-shifted in 2003, just after my twenty-third birthday."

Lizzie stared at him with her mouth open. Nine years was a lifetime – we'd be in our twenties if we ended up here that long.

"But... I don't get it... How did you end up a lord?" Lizzie finally said.

"Ah," Robbie said with a smile. "That was a case of being in the right place at the right time and meeting the most wonderful woman."

"Who?" I asked and popped another caramelised carrot in my mouth.

"Well, she's now my wife..."

"You're married?" Lizzie said, nearly spitting her mouthful of casserole back on to her plate.

Robbie nodded. "I'm married to my lovely Katherine, the previous Lord of Towcester's daughter and we have our four-year-old son, Edward – an absolute adorable terror – an eighteen-month-old daughter, Anne, and another one on the way."

"So your whole life is here." My plate was clean. I put my spoon down and leant back in my chair. "But we're just children and female, we've got no chance."

"Actually I'm a teenager," Lizzie said. "And anyway, what has being female got to do with it?"

"It's the fifteenth century, Lizzie, I don't think girls were treated very well."

"That's so sexist."

Robbie smiled and reached across the table and took one of our hands in his. "Life is tough if you're female, that's true. And yes my whole life is here but only because I chose to come back."

"What do you mean, 'come back'?" My hand tensed in his.

Lizzie looked at me and then at Robbie. "You mean you got back home?"

Chapter Nine

"Initially I was here for about a year. I survived everything the seasons threw at me. I struggled to stay alive at times let alone be warm or fed. I found work with a landowner in Dunstable and although the work was hard I managed to earn a bit and have a roof over my head. I was a quick learner, intelligent, trustworthy and soon became the Lord of Dunstable's confidant and right-hand man. I dressed better, I ate and drank better and then on a hunting trip to Towcester I met the then lord and his daughter Katherine."

"But how did you get back to your own time?" Lizzie asked, leaning forwards.

"I'd been sent on an errand to London and got caught up in a fight early in the morning. Lord Dunstable wasn't with me but I was protecting his name and property. I was punched, I remember falling to the ground, and then everything shifted... just like the first time. What was happening when you two were time-shifted?"

Lizzie bit her lip and glanced at me.

"We were having an argument," I said.

Robbie nodded and banged his fist on the table. "Exactly, there seems to be some sort of conflict."

"What happened after you got time-shifted back?" I asked.

"I ended up – still in my fifteenth-century clothes, mind – on a residential road in London somewhere just south of the Thames. It was early morning so luckily there weren't many people about. But I got strange looks wandering about. I passed it off by saying I'd been to a fancy dress party the night before."

"So if you got back home, how... why did you come back again?" Lizzie asked.

"But I wasn't exactly home."

Lizzie frowned.

"I'd been time-shifted to 1996..."

"I'm confused," Lizzie said. "You said you were time-shifted the first time in 2003?"

"Exactly. I found myself in a time I'd already lived through. My sixteen-year-old self was in school taking GCSEs, and everything I had in 2003 – which admittedly wasn't much – had gone. Even things like my name and national insurance number belonged to my sixteen-year-old self and not to me."

I hunched forwards, my shoulders tense. "So it was just luck you were time-shifted to the future but then you ended up in a time you'd already lived through..."

The door creaked open and footsteps pattered across the flagstones.

"Papa!" A curly haired boy launched himself at Robbie. Robbie laughed and grabbed the boy around the waist and lifted him on to his knee.

"This is Edward," he said, and ruffled his son's hair.

Edward's big blue eyes watched us from beneath his golden curls.

"Did your mother send you away?" Robbie asked. Edward nodded. "Were you being naughty?" Edward shook his head violently, making his curls bounce. Robbie smiled and looked at Lizzie and then me. "I'd best put this little chap to bed and see how Katherine is, and I'm sure now you've eaten you'll want to freshen up. I'll get my housekeeper to find some suitable clothing for you."

He lifted Edward off his knee, scraped back his chair and stood up. "Lead the way, Edward."

The only light in the room was from the fire. Outside the Great Hall windows was darkness although it was probably only early evening still. We followed Robbie into the hallway, which was now lit by candles. Edward bounded up the stairs and disappeared. The first-floor floorboards creaked as Robbie led us down a long corridor. A servant curtsied as we went by. At the end of the corridor were three closed doors. Robbie opened the one on our left.

"This can be your room, Lizzie," he said. We poked our heads in. The sight of a four-poster bed was as good as the feeling on Christmas morning. "Maisie, your room is just opposite, but I want to show you something first."

We moved back out into the corridor and Robbie reached beneath his tunic and pulled out a key tied round his neck with string. He unlocked the end door and tucked the key back beneath his clothing. He ushered us into the room. There was a writing desk in front of a shuttered window, a four-poster bed in one corner and two chests of drawers against the other wall.

"I don't let anyone come in here."

I couldn't see why; there wasn't anything special in here. Lizzie caught my eye and I shrugged. I wandered over to the desk. There was a quill and ink and papers scattered all over the top. Stacked next to the window was a row of books. I didn't think anything of it until I read some of the titles: *The War of the Roses*; *The Kingmaker*. "I don't understand?"

"You haven't seen anything yet." Robbie opened the top drawer of the chest nearest the door. Lizzie gasped. I left the books and peered over her shoulder. The drawer was full of familiar things: Lemsip boxes, plasters, paracetamol, deodorant, perfume bottles, aftershave, razors, toothpaste...

"You brought this stuff back?" I asked.

"I'll explain everything soon enough but first I must go to Katherine. You'll find hot water in a bowl in your rooms and help yourselves to whatever you need from in here. Oh, and I thought you might like these," Robbie said as he reached the door. Something whizzed across the room and I caught a fun-sized Mars bar in my hand. "Close the door behind you when you leave."

As soon as Robbie left we both ripped open the mini Mars bars and stuffed them in our mouths. The sugary sweetness filled my mouth.

"That is *so* good," Lizzie said through a mouthful of chocolate.

"It's the best thing ever."

Lizzie picked out a red toothbrush from the drawer and a pack of paracetamol. "This is mad."

"I've never been so excited at the thought of cleaning my teeth and getting a wash."

"Why did he bring back so much stuff?"

I chose a green toothbrush and grabbed toothpaste, a bar of soap and deodorant. "Because he's not planning on ever going back again."

~

I closed the door of my room and leant against it. Alone at last. The bedroom was large with a four-poster bed opposite a fireplace with a newly lit fire that spat and crackled. On my right was a chest of drawers with a basin and jug of water on it. I dumped my handful of toiletries next to the basin. I washed my face with warm water, brushed my teeth and sprayed deodorant. The bed looked straight out of a National Trust house and I was half-expecting to see a sign on it forbidding me to touch the covers. But it was 1471. I took a run up and launched myself on to the bed. It was surprisingly soft and bouncy. I lay down and listened to the silence of the house with only the wind occasionally rattling the windowpanes. Moonlight squeezed through a gap in the heavy curtains. I closed my eyes and imagined I was home, but there was no loud music playing in Ollie's room, no laughter or cooking smells coming from downstairs and so my daydream was lost. I curled my arms around a pillow and cried.

~

Robbie's housekeeper found us both a clean dress in a grey scratchy fabric.

"I hate it," Lizzie said tugging at the hem as she met me outside our rooms. "I want my jeans and Uggs. I'll die if anyone sees me like this."

"Like who? Who's going to see you or even care that you look like a fifteenth-century peasant?"

"I care."

"At least it's warm."

Downstairs one of the servants directed us to a room off the entrance hall. It was cosy compared to the Great Hall and the warmth from the fire filled the room. The servant came back a minute later holding two cups and handed them to us.

"Warm ale," she said. "Keeps the chills away."

She was pale with a thin nose and bushy eyebrows. She didn't look much older than twenty but then she wasn't wearing make-up so it was difficult to tell.

"Lord Robert will be with you shortly," she said, motioning to the chairs next to the fire.

"Warm ale?" Lizzie said when the woman left the room. She sniffed it before taking a sip. She rolled her eyes. "Ah that's so good."

Under the circumstances I thought Lizzie would like anything after drinking river water. I took a sip. It was warm, slightly spicy and delicious. It reminded me of mulled wine at Christmas.

Instead of sitting on the chairs we sprawled out on a soft rug in front of the fire and drank our ale in silence. I could hardly keep my eyes open.

The door clicked open and Robbie appeared. "Feeling better?"

I sat up cross-legged on the rug. "Much better, thanks. I never thought I'd miss soap and toothpaste so much."

Robbie sat on one of the chairs next to us. "Katherine is resting now and Edward and Anne have gone to bed so we can talk without being interrupted. So shoot: what do you want to ask?"

"Don't you miss home?" I asked.

He shrugged. "I miss certain things; a good curry and pint of beer down my local. I miss cigarettes as tobacco has yet to be discovered and brought back from the Americas, but that can't be a bad thing for my health. I'd love to go to a gig and listen to good music or watch the latest blockbuster and stuff my face with popcorn. Oh and technology to make everyday life easier: the internet, my mobile, simple things like a kettle. But I have a good life... a better life here."

Lizzie frowned. "But what about your family and friends?"

"I was twenty-three when I first time-shifted. I was living in a damp studio flat in London, doing a job I hated. As for family, my mum left when I was seven and my dad couldn't wait to kick me out as soon as I was old enough. It was a rubbish life but I don't want pity because now I have a house, a wife, a son and daughter and feel like I belong here."

"But what if you get ill," Lizzie said. "I mean like really ill... not something you can just take a

Lemsip for."

"When my time is up, it's up," he replied. "I'd rather have a good and short life than a long and miserable one. But you two are young and have the whole of your lives ahead of you and families worried sick about you, so I'll see what I can do to get you home." He stood and topped up our ale from the jug in front of the fireplace. "Let me show you something else." He walked over to a bookshelf and started hunting for something.

Lizzie swirled her drink around. "How could he like living here?" she whispered.

"He fell in love, that's why," I replied under my breath. "And not everyone's fortunate enough to have parents who care about them or a family villa in Portugal..."

"You just love having a dig, don't you?"

"Makes a change from you having a go."

"Ha ha!" Robbie said. He turned back to us with a piece of rolled up parchment and a 1996 AA road map. "There's a trick to time-shifting," he said. "It's possible to get back to your own time but you have to be in *exactly* the right place at the right time."

"What do you mean by *exactly*?" I asked.

He opened the road map on the London page and spread the parchment out next to it with a hand-drawn map on it.

"The first time I went back – or forward should I say – I ended up in 1996, seven years too early. Time-shifting doesn't happen to everyone – the first time it happened to me I was with a girlfriend in Warwick but only I ended up here – although it was 1464 at the time. It's amazing that both of you were time-shifted."

"But it's not just us who were time-shifted," I said. "My best friend Danny was too."

"But if he's not with you..."

"He's with Warwick's army heading to Barnet, which is where we were going when you found us."

Robbie looked sharply at me. "He's with the army?"

I nodded. "I take it that's not good."

He traced his finger along his hand-drawn map from Warwick down to Barnet.

"The Battle of Barnet takes place on the 14th April. It's the 11th today. You'd better hope your friend keeps a low profile and doesn't do anything stupid."

"We have to find him."

"I can't let you go to Barnet, it's too dangerous."

"We're going anyway," I said. "Even if you don't help us."

"But if it's too dangerous..." Lizzie said.

"If you were with the army, Lizzie," I said, "wouldn't you want us to save you?"

"I guess so."

"Then what are we waiting for!" I stood up. "We're wasting time."

Robbie laughed. "It's dark and raining if you hadn't noticed. You'll wait until morning and start off early and refreshed and I'll ride with you as far as Dunstable. But I suggest before you go to sleep tonight you read up on the Battle of Barnet."

"Fine. Great. We're going to go and save Danny," Lizzie said, scowling at me. "But how do we get back *home*?"

Robbie turned the hand-drawn map around to face us. He ran his finger along a line that went from Warwick to London. "As far as I can tell, anywhere along this line puts you at risk from being time-shifted. That's what I've figured out from going backwards and forwards through time. Warwick, Dunstable and the city of London have all been hotspots for me and there's no reason to believe they won't be for you either. The further north you are the further back in time you'll be shifted. Barnet is on the line too. But there's a second timeline that runs from Cornwall to the east coast and cuts through south London and that'll be the one that gets you home." He drew a black cross on the map. "So to have any chance of getting back to your own time you have to be at this spot south of the Thames."

"Or what?" Lizzie asked.

"Or you'll end up in a different time altogether."

Chapter Ten

I woke to a cockerel crowing. I was warm and cosy all snuggled up in bed and for a moment I believed I was at home on our farm. I almost imagined I could smell bacon frying downstairs. I waited until my eyes adjusted to the gloomy room. Yesterday morning I'd woken up achy and cold beneath a tree and now I was sleeping on the softest bed ever.

I wanted to leave early to try and close the gap between Warwick's army and us. I swung my legs out of bed and padded over to the window and drew back the thick curtains. Grey light flooded in. I squinted but could only see trees poking through the mist. It didn't look very inviting and half of me wanted to get back into bed. Instead, I cleaned my teeth, washed my face and started to put on the clean clothes that had been laid out for me on the chest at the foot of the bed. Overnight I'd gone from looking like a peasant to a lady. The pale green dress was a bit too big with a high waist, square neckline and long, tight sleeves that covered my hands. There was a pair of soft leather boots next to the chest. I picked up a cap with a turned up brim, put it on and went to the window to see my reflection. In the billowing dress I looked totally ridiculous.

My bedroom door slammed open and Lizzie stormed in red-faced and wearing a flattering gold version of the dress I was in. Hers had a jewel at the centre of the waistband.

"What am I supposed to do with this?" she said, waving a jewelled piece of fabric at me.

"Come on in why don't you," I said.

"Aaargh!" She paced across my room pulling at her dress. "I can't even walk in this."

"Chill out, Lizzie, it's just a dress," I said. "I'm the tomboy remember. Anyway we can hardly walk around in trousers."

"Tights. The men wear tights and the women wear poncey dresses."

"I think you look really pretty in it."

"Oh," she said, turning awkwardly to face me. "Thanks."

She *was* really pretty. Her hair was clean and brushed and lay straight against her shoulders. Mine was a mass of curls that bobbed up and down every time I moved.

"I'm hungry," I said to break the silence.

"Me too."

~

Breakfast was a huge bowl of porridge in front of the fire in the Great Hall. Afterwards we went outside to find Robbie.

"Morning," I said as we joined him at the stables. It was misty, cold and damp and I was very glad we'd spent the night indoors.

"Well, don't you two look like ladies of the manor?"

Lizzie scowled and I curtsied and giggled at the ridiculousness of our situation. We followed Robbie into the stables and I immediately felt at home with the comforting smell of straw and horses. There were two ponies tied up at the end of the stable: a beautiful grey one and a chestnut one with a naughty gleam in its eye.

"Have either of you two ridden before?" Robbie asked. He stroked the nose of the grey pony and it let out a gentle snort.

"Uh, uh," Lizzie said, shaking her head and not going anywhere near the ponies.

"I have. We've got horses on our farm. My dad always says I learnt to ride before I could walk."

"Excellent," Robbie said and handed me the reins of the chestnut pony. "This is Goliath and Lizzie yours is Zeus." Lizzie was pale. "Don't worry he's a real softy, it's Goliath who's trouble," he said winking at me.

We led Goliath and Zeus into the yard. One of the stable boys was saddling Robbie's horse.

"James!" Robbie yelled and a boy not much older than me shot out into the yard.

"Yes, my Lord."

"Saddle these ponies and get my guests' provisions ready."

The boy took the reins from us and led the ponies over to Robbie's horse.

"So Lizzie," Robbie said. "You've never ridden before."

"Never going to either."

"Is that so," he said and chuckled. "That's fine if you want to get there three days too late. The battle begins in two days and if you ride you might just have a chance of finding your friend."

"He's not my friend."

Robbie frowned. "Even so, he needs your help."

The greatest moment was watching Lizzie ride for the first time. She refused any help from Robbie or the stable boy and after a struggle managed to scramble on to Zeus. He was well behaved and stood perfectly still for her so she didn't topple off. Once up she sat hunched over his mane, her knuckles white where she gripped the edge of the saddle.

"Now sit with your back straight and hold on to the reins rather than the saddle."

I was glad Robbie was teaching her as there was no way she'd have ever listened to me. Anyway, it was far more fun watching. Robbie walked Zeus around the yard and Lizzie managed to stay upright.

"Keep the stirrups on your toes and your heels down," Robbie said as he stepped up the pace around the yard.

"Wait, wait, slow down!" Lizzie shouted as she began to hunch forwards again. "I'm going to fall!"

"No you're not!" Robbie said. "Keep your back straight and heels down."

The stable boy led Goliath over to me. "You want to ride him, Miss?"

I nodded and he handed me the reins. I stroked Goliath's velvety nose and he snorted. "You're going to be a good boy and take us all the way to Barnet," I whispered. He was the same build and height as my pony, Noodle. I would imagine I was on a trek in the Brecon Beacons instead of riding towards battle. I gathered up the bottom of my dress, put my foot in the stirrup and swung myself on to Goliath. I reined him in as he was impatient to get going and waited for Robbie and Lizzie to pass by. Lizzie was concentrating so hard her tongue was sticking out. I kicked Goliath and we set off at a trot across the yard.

"How do you do that?" Lizzie asked as I passed her doing a rising trot. There was nothing like a bit of competition for Lizzie to want to learn.

~

It was still early morning and misty by the time we set off. We had saddlebags filled with water and food, kindling to start a fire and hooded cloaks to wear at night or to use as blankets, plus a two-man tent Robbie took with him whenever he travelled in case he time-shifted. Edward came out of the house to say goodbye and I caught a glimpse of Robbie's wife waving to us from a first-floor window. Robbie blew her a kiss and then reined his horse away from the house. We followed the road that led out of Towcester and passed the spot where we'd met Robbie only the day before. Robbie had Lizzie's pony on a lead and when we were out of sight of the town he picked up the pace. Lizzie clung to Zeus as we trotted along. Robbie shouted: "You're doing great! Keep your back straight!"

We passed horse-drawn carts loaded with food, barrels and people. We slowed down when we got to villages and the road became busy with people and horses. There was talk of soldiers and Warwick and Edward IV. Robbie stopped to speak to a merchant selling trinkets at the side of the road and asked him what he'd seen or heard.

The morning mist burnt away and by the middle of the day the sky was blue and I was hot from riding. I was also saddle sore and beginning to wonder how Lizzie was coping. We stopped for lunch by a stream and sat on our cloaks in the grass.

"We're making good time," Robbie said, pulling out bread, cheese and a pie from one of his saddlebags. "How're you doing, Lizzie?"

"Just fine," she said, slumping on the ground and wincing.

"We'll make a rider out of you yet," he laughed. He handed us each a slab of homemade pie and I tucked in greedily. It tasted of beef and onions and ale and we didn't talk again until we'd eaten every last crumb.

After lunch we picked up the pace on a straight open road. Most people in carts or on foot seemed to be heading in the opposite direction to us, which worried me about what we'd find up ahead. Unlike Lizzie, who had to spend all her time concentrating on riding and staying on, I got the chance to look at the places we went through: the farmhands at work in the fields, thatched roofs being repaired and children my age begging at the side of the road. We were riding along happily and even Lizzie seemed to have relaxed a bit when a rabbit ran in front of Robbie's horse and made him rear. Robbie dropped the leading rope and a startled Zeus took off down the road at a canter.

"Turn him towards the trees!" I shouted after Lizzie.

"You better go get her," Robbie said as he fought for control of his horse. I kicked Goliath and galloped after Zeus. Lizzie lost her footing in the stirrups and clung to his neck. She screamed as Zeus suddenly slowed and she slipped to the left and landed with a thud in the grass at the side of the road. I reined Goliath in, jumped down and crouched next to Lizzie.

"Are you okay?"

"What do you think?" she said. Tears streamed down her face. "My bum really hurts."

"Well you did land on it quite hard."

"It's not funny."

"I'm really not laughing."

"Congratulations, Lizzie," Robbie said, riding past us and taking hold of Zeus' reins. "You've had your first fall. Riding will be a piece of cake from now on."

"I'm not getting back up on that thing." Lizzie folded her arms.

"It really isn't that much further," Robbie said, taking her hand and pulling her to her feet.

~

We reached the outskirts of Dunstable just as the light was beginning to fade. A church steeple and chimney tops poked through the trees.

"I'm afraid I can't go with you any further," Robbie said. "I live in permanent fear of being time-shifted away from my family and the chances of that happening are greatly increased between Dunstable and London. I can't take the risk."

The thought of being on our own again filled me with fear. I'd never felt anything like it. A sleepless night before a test at school or even being sent to the headmaster's office was nothing compared to what I was feeling right now. I nodded but couldn't say anything because of the lump forming in my throat. Lizzie wiped her eyes with the sleeve of her dress.

Robbie took hold of our ponies' reins so the three of us were facing each other in a triangle.

"There's only one road between here and London and that goes straight through Barnet. Once you find your friend, don't waste any time, head straight to London and get south of the river to give yourselves the best possible chance of getting home."

"What about Goliath and Zeus?" I asked.

"They're yours for as long as you need them. Once you time-shift they'll find their way back home." He let go of our reins and turned his horse to go but then twisted in his saddle so he faced us. "Just be careful who you trust."

"What do you mean?" I asked.

"Nothing," he said, reining his horse away from us. "Just be careful."

Chapter Eleven

"What does he mean be careful? Be careful of who?" Lizzie wiped away the tears streaming down her face.

I watched Robbie riding away until he was out of sight. "I don't know."

"This sucks."

I took hold of the rope Robbie had been leading Zeus with. "Come on, let's find this inn."

We rode the last half a mile to Dunstable at a gentle pace. Tucked in my saddlebag was a letter from Robbie stamped with his Towcester seal ready for me to give to the Dunstable innkeeper — a friend of Katherine's family — with payment for a night's lodgings. Dunstable was smaller than Towcester with just the main road to London cutting through the town. With the sun so low in the sky, I wanted to be inside before it got completely dark.

"That must be the place," Lizzie said, pointing ahead.

It was the biggest building in Dunstable and it at least looked welcoming with lanterns hanging outside the door. We rode past and found a lane to the side of the inn with stabling at the end. I dismounted and tied Goliath's reins to a cart filled with hay propped up against the inn wall. Lizzie managed to dismount on her own and I tied Zeus up too. I took the letter from my saddlebag and patted Goliath before we walked round to the inn door. All I could see inside was a roaring fire and it took a while for my eyes to adjust to the gloom. I smelt woodsmoke and heard men talking and laughing. We moved further into the room and the men quietened down. I felt everyone's eyes on us. Lizzie kept so close to me it was as if we were super-glued together.

"Welcome, guests!" a voice boomed across the inn. I expected to see a tall, imposing man but the voice belonged to a short, round man with plump cheeks. He looked friendly enough pouring ale into pitchers behind the bar.

"I take it you're the innkeeper," I said, sounding way more confident than I felt. I handed him Robbie's letter. He looked at the seal and then at us, his jolly face pinching into a frown that lasted less than a second before his smile returned.

"Not another of Robert and Katherine's waifs and strays," he said with a chuckle.

"Their what?" Lizzie asked sharply.

"You mean Rob... Lord Robert has done this before... there've been other people before us?"

"Once, but not for a while. Last couple weren't half strange mind. The woman had flame red hair, fancy that. Robert knew she'd be safe enough with us, no talk of witchcraft here." He folded the letter and tucked it inside his shirt. "What brings you two this way?"

"The Battle of..." Lizzie began.

"Family," I said quickly. "In London. That's

where we're headed."

The innkeeper nodded and Lizzie bit her lip.

"My wife will show you to a room."

"Our ponies are tied up outside..."

"I'll see to it my son puts them in the stable for the night."

The innkeeper's wife was shorter, but just as round as her husband. We followed her up the stairs and along a hallway. She stopped at the furthest door and unlocked it. "It's nothing fancy but you should be comfortable."

There was a large bed – just the one, so we'd have to share – a washstand and a chest of drawers. We were getting used to the basics, like weeing in a hole.

"You girls hungry?"

We nodded.

"Make yourselves at home and I'll bring you up some stew." She bustled out of the room.

"It's not like we've got anything to unpack," Lizzie said, slumping on to the bed. "Which side do you want?"

"I'm not fussed."

"Good, because I want to sleep on the side closest to the door."

I went to the window and peered out. Directly below was the cart of hay and the innkeeper's son untying our ponies. He led them along the lane to the stables and I watched until they were out of sight.

Lizzie had kicked off her boots and lay on the left side of the bed staring up at the ceiling. "I wonder what's happening back home?" she said. "Do you reckon the police are out looking for us?"

I sat on the bed next to her. "I guess so. We've been gone for four days."

"Maybe there'll be a Facebook page dedicated to us?"

"Are you worried you're missing out on your fifteen minutes of fame?"

"I don't want to be famous for being a missing person."

"But you want to be famous?"

"Don't you?"

"Not really, no."

"So," Lizzie said. "What *do* you want to do when you're older?"

"I want to work with animals. On our farm, or maybe be a vet."

"I want to carry on acting, go to drama school and do more film and TV work, like when I was in *Harry Potter*, but not just as an extra. I've been put forward for four days' filming next month on *Doctor Who* in Cardiff, which will be amazing."

"It helps that your dad's a TV producer though..."

"Beef stew," the innkeeper's wife said, barging in. She placed two steaming bowls of food on the chest. My stomach rumbled.

"I'll leave you girls to it then," she said, flattening the front of her dress down. "I'm going to lock the door for the night – young girls like yourselves travelling alone." She tutted and crossed herself.

I didn't like the thought of being a prisoner inside the room but there was no way I'd leave the door of a Travelodge unlocked, let alone a strange room in an inn in 1471.

"We need to leave really early in the morning though," I said.

"I'll unlock the door before sunrise."

~

Something woke me up. Maybe it was the innkeeper's wife unlocking our door. It was dark and Lizzie was still asleep, breathing loudly next to me. Voices came from somewhere inside the inn and none of them belonged to the innkeeper's wife. A door banged. The voices were getting nearer. Footsteps thudded on the landing. Lizzie stirred.

"Wake up, Lizzie!" I elbowed her in the ribs. "Something's going on."

I jumped out of bed and put my ear to the door.

"Which room are they in?" a deep voice asked.

"I'm not sure, my wife dealt with them," the innkeeper said. Another door slammed open. They were working their way down the corridor.

"Well wake your wife up." This time it was a woman's voice.

Lizzie rubbed her eyes. "What's going on?"

"Shush!" I held a finger to my lips. "I've got a bad feeling about this."

"About what?"

"There are people out there," I pointed towards the door. "Looking for someone."

"So?"

84

"What if the someone is us?"

Lizzie frowned, opened her mouth to say something and then glanced towards the door.

"Mary!" the innkeeper shouted. "Wake up!"

There was another thud out on the landing. Lizzie scrambled out of bed, tugged on her boots, grabbed her dress and shoved it on over her tunic top and tights. I did the same.

"Why would anyone be after us?" Lizzie asked, pacing across the room. A door slammed closed and shook the floorboards. "They're in the next room," she whispered.

I looked around. The room was small with nowhere to hide. I yanked the window open. The lane was deserted, just the hay cart below... Our bedroom door handle rattled. Lizzie staggered back into the room.

"This room's locked," the deep-voiced man said.

"They must be in there," the woman said. "Open it."

"My wife's got the keys. Mary, hurry up!"

"Jump down on to the hay below," I said, pushing Lizzie to the window.

The door rattled violently now.

"You have to be joking." Lizzie shook her head and gripped the side of the window. There was no time. I pushed her out of the way, wriggled through and manoeuvred myself on to the window ledge.

"If I don't splatter and die then follow me." I launched myself out of the first-floor window and landed with a thud in the scratchy straw below. I rolled off the cart and put my feet on firm ground. No broken bones, just a bit sore. "I'm okay!"

Lizzie clambered on to the window ledge, took a deep breath and jumped. She landed in the straw with her dress caught up around her waist. I grabbed her outstretched hand and pulled her to her feet.

"Now what?" she whispered.

I kicked away a piece of wood wedged under the wheel and pushed the cart until it was no longer beneath the window. "We get Zeus and Goliath."

There was a crash from above as they finally broke our door down. I motioned for Lizzie to follow and, keeping to the shadows of the inn, we ran towards the stables. I lifted the stable latch and the door creaked open. It was still the middle of the night but our only option was to leave and continue our journey. I didn't fancy finding out what these people wanted. Zeus and Goliath were in the second stable. Goliath let out a gentle whinny when he saw me.

"Good boy." I opened their stable door and led them out while Lizzie gathered up the saddles and bags.

I realised the only way out of Dunstable was on the road that went past the inn. "Pass me a saddle," I whispered. "We're going to have to ride out of here. Fast."

Lizzie didn't argue. She did as I asked stopping both the ponies from moving as I threw the saddles on and yanked the girths tight. I gave her a leg-up on to Zeus and then clambered on to Goliath.

"You ready?" I took hold of the rope Robbie had used to lead her.

She nodded.

"Once we get to the main road we turn left and ride until Dunstable is out of sight. Got it?"

"Got it."

Chapter Twelve

I gripped the reins and set off at a trot down the lane. I wanted to go faster but I didn't want to risk Lizzie losing her balance and falling off again as we rounded the corner.

In front of the inn a hooded figure holding a flaming torch stood next to two horses. Just as the figure turned and caught sight of us I kicked Goliath into a canter and we raced away through Dunstable.

"Maybe they're not looking for us!" Lizzie shouted.

The wind stung my eyes and whipped my hair. We galloped past the last house in Dunstable and out on to the open road.

"We're okay now, aren't we?" Lizzie looked really pale in the moonlight.

I glanced at the dark road behind us. An orangey glow bobbing up and down in the distance caught my attention. "Oh no."

"What do you mean 'Oh no'?"

"They're following us."

We thundered along the road lined with skeletal trees but ahead was just darkness. My heart thumped so hard against my ribs I could barely breathe. I didn't dare look back. They were on horses and we were on ponies and eventually they would catch up.

"We need to hide." I glanced back. The flaming

torches were getting closer, flickering through the trees. "We don't have much time."

The wood loomed against the moonlit sky. I turned Goliath towards the trees and tightened my grip on the rope attached to Zeus. "Hold on!" I said.

Branches whipped and tore at our clothes and skin as we entered the wood. We were forced to slow down. There was no clear path and the trees were dense. We headed away from the road, deeper into the wood. The only noise was the crunch of twigs under hooves, the ponies' snorts and our breathing, loud in the darkness. I twisted in the saddle. I couldn't see anything behind us. Could we be that lucky and have lost them? No, there was the familiar orange glow flickering through the trees moving parallel to us. Did that mean they were still on the road?

Goliath stopped and I was thrown forwards but I managed to grab hold of his mane to steady myself. Lizzie's leading rope slipped from my hand as Zeus kept moving.

"Maisie?"

"I'm here, don't worry."

There was a splash and Zeus walked into a stream shimmering in the moonlight. Now I understood why Goliath had stopped. I kicked him but he wouldn't budge. His hooves were planted firmly at the edge of the stream.

"Maisie!" Lizzie's voice was high-pitched and way too loud. She was on the other side of the stream now. "I can't stop."

"Turn him away from the stream and into a tree."

I dismounted, grabbed Goliath's reins and splashed into the water, gasping at the cold. I pulled at his reins but he was stubborn and still wouldn't move. Lizzie had come to a stop; I could see the gleam of Zeus' grey coat not far away.

"Come on, Goliath," I said, stroking his velvety nose. A crack of a branch somewhere in the wood made him look up. Maybe he could smell my fear because with another tug on his reins he joined me in the stream. Lizzie's hands shook as she handed me the leading rope.

"They're coming," I whispered.

Still on foot, I led both ponies into the undergrowth. A fallen tree leaning against a thick trunk seemed a good place to hide behind. I motioned for Lizzie to dismount and she slid off Zeus and thudded on to damp leaves. I loosely tied the ponies' reins to a branch and hoped we were hidden enough behind the tree trunk. The flicker of torch flames along with the sound of branches snapping and the crunch of hooves heavy on the ground got closer.

"We're not even sure they came this way," the deep voice of the man from the inn said.

"I saw the grey pony," the woman replied.

Now they were just the other side of the stream. I held my breath as the two riders dismounted. Even Zeus and Goliath stayed perfectly still.

"We've lost them," the woman said, shoving

her hands into the man's chest. "I told you we should have gone to the inn as soon as we knew they were there."

"Don't start." The man stepped forward and in the moonlight beneath his hood I could see dark hair, sunken eyes and a beard. "They can't have gone far," he said and stopped at the edge of the stream.

I hardly dared breathe in case he heard me. Lizzie hunched against me, completely still. If only they would walk downstream a bit so they weren't standing opposite us. Goliath tugged at the rein tied to the tree and stomped the ground. The man's eyes shot in our direction and our cover was blown. We had no choice, either stay and be caught or leg it and hope we could lose them in the wood.

"Run!" I hissed in Lizzie's ear. Without waiting for her to reply, I turned and started running in the opposite direction to the riders. Lizzie had listened; I could hear her panting behind me. I crashed through the wood, branches snapping at my legs. My feet kept catching the bottom of my dress and I couldn't run as fast as normal. I just hoped it was fast enough.

A scream.

I slowed. There were no other footsteps following me.

"Maisie!" Lizzie's voice was distant. "Help!" she screamed, and then her next cry was muffled as if someone had clamped a hand over her mouth.

I stopped and listened. There was definitely no one following me. I strained to make out their voices but I couldn't hear what they were saying. If I went back they would capture me too. I peered through the darkness at the trees surrounding me. I was in the middle of the wood and I had no idea which direction the road was. I had no choice but to go back. I couldn't leave Lizzie alone with them. We had Danny to find. I was wasting time thinking things through. I retraced my steps, slower this time, and quietly. In the distance Lizzie started screaming again. I had no idea what I'd actually do when I reached them. Despite having only run for no more than a minute, the walk back felt as if it went on forever. When I heard trickling water I slowed down and crept forward from tree to tree watching for the dark figures. I caught sight of Zeus and Goliath first, still tied to the fallen tree trunk. Lizzie was slumped on the ground and the two horses the man and woman had been riding were grazing across the other side of the stream. But there was no sign of the riders themselves.

"*Lizzie,*" I whispered.

Her head shot in my direction. Her face was pale and she clutched at her arm.

I stepped out from behind the tree. "What happened?" I asked. "Where did they go?"

"The man caught me and you kept running," she said in between sobs. "He held on to my arm really hard and yanked my chin up until I was looking at him and then said to the woman, 'we've got the wrong one'."

"That doesn't make any sense."

Lizzie glared at me. "I'm only telling you what he said."

"But where have they gone?"

"Give me a chance and I'll tell you." She rubbed her arm and winced. "Three other people, a man and two women, then appeared out of nowhere. And I mean from nowhere. The man – he had this weird scar on his palm – pulled the bearded bloke off me and they all started fighting except one of the new women who stayed with me."

"What did they want with us?"

"How should I know, they were all fighting and shouting at each other."

"This new woman, she must have said something to you?"

"I was scared. I was too busy trying to get away; I wasn't listening to her," she said, wiping tears from her face with the sleeve of her dress. "And anyway they all disappeared."

"What do you mean they disappeared?"

"They didn't *just* disappear," she said, scrambling to her feet. "I think they time-shifted."

"What, all of them together, just time-shifted?"

"That's what I said."

"It makes no sense."

"What part of the last few days has made any sense? It's 1471 and we're in the past being chased by strange hooded people on horseback." She walked over to Zeus and stroked his mane.

"Now can we please get back on the road? This wood is freaking me out."

As I untied our ponies, every creak of the trees in the wind and every rustle in the undergrowth seemed as loud as thunder. "There must have been something you noticed about them or something they said?"

"None of them looked like they were from the fifteenth century and I'm pretty sure they weren't from our time either," she said and chewed her lip. "Now can you just shut up about it so we can get back on the road."

Chapter Thirteen

Lizzie trailed silently behind me as we picked our way through the wood on foot, leading Zeus and Goliath and heading in what we hoped was the right direction. I was glad it was a clear night. The moon shone brighter through the trees thinning ahead, guiding us back to the road. I kept glancing behind, certain I could hear footsteps and expecting to see the dark riders following us. Only when we reached the deserted road did my breathing begin to slow.

"Maybe we should go back to the inn," Lizzie said.

"Did you not hear what the innkeeper said? They were helping those riders. What if the innkeeper and his wife were the ones who let the riders know we were there?"

"Why would they do that? Why would Robbie have let us go to the inn if it wasn't safe? He was the one who told us to be careful."

"Like you said, nothing makes sense." I pointed towards Dunstable. "That direction is the past. This direction is home." I put my foot in a stirrup and swung myself on to Goliath.

Lizzie didn't argue about keeping a fast pace along the road. It felt safer that way, moving too quickly for anyone to be able to creep out of the wood and grab us. I was aware of every sound and I kept checking behind us that no one was following. We cantered along in silence until we left the wood behind. It wasn't unusual for Lizzie to be quiet but she was completely silent. Maybe she was just concentrating on staying on Zeus but she looked as pale and tense as Mum had when the doctor at the hospital told her Grandad had suffered a heart attack. I shrugged the thought off. Lizzie was always moody and rarely smiled, so what did I expect after she'd been captured by people who then time-shifted away in front of her? But if they could time-shift like we had at Warwick Castle, where were they from and more importantly what time were they from? Why would anyone be trying to capture us anyway and how did they know we were at the inn? I hoped Robbie and his family were okay. More than anything I wanted to find Danny and get home.

Each wood and village we rode through was a step closer to Barnet and Danny. We'd ridden for miles before it started to get light and a watery sun appeared on the horizon. With the comfort of daylight, the night's adventures became a blur. I couldn't really believe what had happened. I slowed the ponies to a walk as we had all day to ride half the distance we'd ridden the day before with Robbie. The slower pace gave me time to notice our surroundings. This was fifteenth-century England we were riding through – I felt a bubble of excitement in my stomach at the thought. Me and Danny wanted to travel the world when we were older and find the last few remote places on the planet to explore. But this was an adventure I couldn't have dreamt of. I only wished Danny was here to share the experience with me rather than Lizzie.

We stopped for lunch on top of a hill just a little way from the road.

"There's hardly anyone about," I said, ripping off a chunk of bread. "Everywhere seems so open and wild."

"It's 1471, what do you expect?"

"I'm just saying." I stood on the edge of the hill and munched on the meat pie Robbie's cook had packed for us. I could see for miles. The London road cut through the green landscape and villages were dotted about. Smoke swirled from chimneys. It was a landscape untouched by pylons or factories or spoilt by big dirty cities and too many people. I could see why Robbie wanted to stay here. I popped the last bit of pie into my mouth and walked back over to where Lizzie sat cross-legged in the grass. It was the easiest afternoon we'd had since we first time-shifted. The sun shone, our stomachs were full and we rode at a steady pace lost in our own thoughts. We passed people on the road, some on horseback, young children playing by the side of the road and plenty of carts travelling between villages.

We rode for the rest of the day. It was good to think we were heading in the right direction and hopefully gaining ground on the army and Danny. They had marched this way already. There were the obvious signs of where they'd made camp for the night: flattened grass spreading out from the roadside and scorched ground and charred wood, the leftovers of campfires. St Albans was the biggest town we'd been through since Dunstable and at the market we overheard talk of the army. We bought bread from a stall beneath the clock tower with the money Robbie had given us.

The sun was beginning to dip in the sky so we didn't hang about in St Albans for long. The London road wound itself past the last few cottages on the outskirts of the town and then we were back in open countryside.

"This must be the heath land Robbie told us about to make sure we're not near the army," I said.

"Let's find somewhere to camp then." Lizzie slid off Zeus and followed me on to the vast expanse of grassland that stretched to the horizon. We didn't want to be too far away from the road but we didn't want to be seen either. We walked in a straight line until the ground dipped. Hidden from the road in its own valley was a large oak tree.

I pointed. "There's our camp site."

We tied the ponies to the tree, took the tent out of Lizzie's saddlebag and laid it out on the ground.

"Have you never camped before?" I asked as I started slotting the poles together while Lizzie read the instructions.

"Only once in France. In a caravan."

"That's a no then."

"Why would Robbie even think of bringing a

tent back?" Lizzie asked.

"He said he takes a tent with him when he travels anywhere he's at risk of being time-shifted, so he has somewhere dry and sheltered to sleep. It's good for us."

"No Maisie, being at home in our own beds would be good for us."

I slotted the last pole in place and moved it under the tree. "Help me put the tent on."

Lizzie grabbed one corner of the canvas and together we lifted it over the poles and straightened it out so it was neat on all sides with the tent flap facing away from the tree.

"If you want to light the gas stove, I'll finish off here." I took the hammer and one of the pegs and started to secure the tent. This would be Danny and me, Ollie and his best friend Ben on our camping trip we'd planned for the summer holidays. We'd talked about going to Ben's uncle's campsite in the Brecon Beacons where Ollie wanted to catch fish from the river to barbecue for dinner. I banged another peg into the ground to secure the back of the tent. There was something exciting about camping just anywhere, not having the comfort of a toilet and shower block. I shivered and pulled my cloak tighter around my shoulders. I wanted food and then sleep before we began the final part of our journey to find Danny.

"Aaargh!" Lizzie shouted from over the other side of the tent. She had the lighter in her hand and a frown on her face. The camping gas stove was unlit. "How do you get this stupid thing to work?"

I dropped the hammer and pegs on the ground, took the lighter from her, turned the switch on the stove and ignited the gas.

Lizzie folded her arms and glared at me. "We *always* eat out on holiday."

One of Robbie's servants had put yesterday's casserole into a caddy for us and I placed it straight over the flame. Lizzie unzipped the tent flap and crawled in. I went back to the tent pegs and hammered the rest of them in. It was getting chilly. The sun was a bleeding mass of red spreading across the sky. Dad always liked a red sky at night, especially when he was harvesting. "Shepherd's delight," he always said.

"What are we supposed to sleep on?" Lizzie shouted from inside the tent.

I warmed my hands over the gas stove and sighed. "Robbie tied blankets on the saddles."

She emerged from the tent, stomped over to Zeus and Goliath and started untying the rolled up blankets. "Is this all we've got to keep us warm?"

"Don't tell me? You usually have thick warm duvets on holiday?"

"We usually go somewhere hot."

The rabbit casserole bubbled and as I stirred it, the smell of herbs and caramelised carrots made my mouth water. "This is ready," I said, taking the caddy off the stove using my extra-long sleeve to stop it burning my hand. "Food will warm us up."

I sat cross-legged on the grass next to Lizzie with the caddy between us. We ate in silence; the only sounds were Zeus and Goliath grazing and us blowing on spoonfuls of food. The warmth of the casserole reminded me of being at Robbie's. I didn't know how we would have coped if he hadn't found us. Even though we'd only known him for a couple of days, I missed him. He was our link to home, the future and everything familiar.

"It's good," I said, taking another mouthful.

Lizzie nodded. The light was dusky and beyond our little campsite darkness had taken over. I hoped there was no one wandering the grassland to discover our twenty-first century tent and stove.

Lizzie blew on another spoonful of food. "You know, there was something really odd about the man and two women who appeared in the wood."

"Like what?"

"I'm not sure, just a feeling," she shrugged. "I was too busy trying to get away to take much in."

"I know. I could hear you screaming a mile off."

"It's just... Oh I don't know..."

"Tell me."

"The woman who had hold of me looked... I dunno she seemed familiar."

"Who did she remind you of?"

Lizzie looked me straight in the face. "You."

"Me?" I laughed.

Lizzie nodded. "Yeah, like your older sister or something... if you had one."

"But it was dark right, and you said you weren't really taking much notice?"

She nodded. "When the rider, the man with the beard, first caught me, I thought he was going to kill me."

"But why? I don't get why they were after us to begin with."

"But the other three they were definitely trying to help me," she said slowly. She played with the remaining spoonful of casserole in the caddy. "The woman who had hold of me, the one I said looked like you, kept saying 'Lizzie, listen...' And then I'd start screaming again."

"Wait!" I grabbed her arm and she stopped scraping the spoon along the bottom of the caddy. "She said *Lizzie* listen?"

"Oh," she said, dropping the spoon and looking at me. "She knew my name."

"But she didn't tell you anything before they time-shifted?"

"No. I don't know. She could have done. I wasn't really listening."

I had goosebumps all over my arms. It was cloudy and the moon was half-hidden giving us very little light to see anything by.

I shivered. "Let's get inside the tent."

I couldn't sleep. I kept thinking about the riders chasing us through the wood and what the woman had been trying to tell Lizzie. How did she know her name? And if they were from the future why were they in the past looking for us? At some point I fell asleep because the next thing I knew it was light. I crawled from beneath the blanket and unzipped the tent, stepped outside and stretched my aching arms and legs. Lizzie was already outside, standing with her hands on her hips looking out on the misty morning.

"Hi," I said, joining her.

"It said in one of Robbie's history books that it was foggy on the morning of the battle."

"You read one of his books?"

"There wasn't anything else to do."

"What time do you think it is?" I asked, straining to see anything through the fog.

"Early. I was awake just before it got light. I didn't sleep well for some reason," she said.

We had bread and cheese for breakfast, packed up the tent and set off on the last part of the journey to Barnet. The road was empty and everywhere was thick with fog so we trotted along gently. We didn't even realise we were going through villages until a house loomed out of the fog at the side of the road. At times I could barely see Goliath's ears. Everywhere was quiet with just the sound of Zeus' and Goliath's hooves on the road, birds twittering in the trees and the occasional cart creaking along loaded with the farmer's produce. I didn't see a sign for Barnet but I figured we must be getting close when Lizzie reined in Zeus.

"Maisie, listen."

It was the sound of men screaming.

Chapter Fourteen

In the eeriness of the cold foggy morning the screams sent shivers through me. I didn't want to ride any further or risk the noise making Zeus bolt. But most of all I didn't actually want to witness what was through the fog. I reined Goliath in and dismounted.

"Let's tie the ponies here and walk," I said.

Together we crept through the damp grass towards the cries, shouts and clang of metal. I wanted to run in the opposite direction but Danny was somewhere among the noise. What if he was injured... what if...? I stopped on the slope.

"What now?" Lizzie turned to face me.

"What if Danny's dead?"

She stared at me with her mouth open. "Don't be stupid. He's twelve. He's too young to die."

With the bloodthirsty noise of battle growing by the second, I couldn't hold back my tears any longer. Tears for Danny, and for Mum, Dad and Ollie streamed down my face, and tears for leaving Robbie behind and for being chased and for being stuck in the past.

Lizzie awkwardly put her arm round me and left it there, heavy on my shoulders. I wiped away my tears with the end of my sleeve.

"We'll find Danny," she said. "He'll be okay, I promise."

Shouts and a clash of swords from somewhere

close made me jump. Lizzie's grip tightened on my shoulder. I couldn't see a thing through the fog but heard a duh duh, duh duh sound like something rolling... something rolling and picking up speed. And then a soldier rolled to a stop in front of us. A dead soldier with a broken sword stuck in his chest. We both screamed and staggered backwards, falling on to the grass.

"This is so not happening," Lizzie whispered as we untangled ourselves from each other and stood up.

"This is so, so wrong." I couldn't take my eyes off the dead soldier, and to think just moments before he'd been alive and fighting for his life. Who would miss him? Parents? A wife? His wide-open eyes freaked me out and I shuddered. "Let's find Danny and get out of here."

We made our way back up the slope, struggling with the heavy fabric of our long dresses. All my muscles ached from riding such a long distance and Lizzie breathed heavily next to me. We reached the top of the hill and looked across the battlefield towards Barnet. Thick white fog obscured almost everything except patches, which revealed snatches of battle: sword fights, overturned carts, slain soldiers and wounded horses. I'd snuck into the barn at home once and watched the vet put down one of our horses but that was nothing compared to the suffering in front of us now.

"We're never going to find him," Lizzie said shaking her head.

"Then we'll have to shout and hope he hears us." I started to pick my way on to the battlefield trying to only step on grass. "Danny!"

"Wait." Lizzie grabbed my arm. "If I was Danny no way would I have stayed among that lot," she said, pointing towards the battlefield. "I'm sure they didn't make children fight."

We retraced our steps and started to walk the perimeter keeping the slope to our left. Lizzie was right. As soon as the battle had begun Danny would have tried to get away. He might have been on the outskirts of the army to begin with and so would be unharmed. I quickened my pace and yelled Danny's name over and over. Everyone we stumbled across was dead or dying. I veered to the left heading even further away from the battle still raging in the distance and the bitter smell of smoke and the stench of blood and sweat and wee. A small dark shape moved through the fog ahead. I held my arm out to stop Lizzie.

"What?"

"I think that might be him."

I took her hand and we crept forwards. The movement came from a figure... a small figure, with his back to us, bending up and down among the bodies surrounding him. I let go of Lizzie's hand and ran towards him. "Danny?"

He turned as I reached him, his dirty face frowning at me. We were inches away from each other and he shoved me away. I stumbled back, my foot landing in something squishy I didn't dare look at.

"Leave me be," the boy growled.

"Do you know Danny? Know where he is?"

The boy looked at me. Tears streaked down his dirty face. He pushed me away and staggered off into the fog.

Lizzie was right behind me as we blindly headed after the boy through the patchy fog towards a cart.

"Danny?" I called.

A small figure appeared from behind the cart.

"Danny?" I called again and the boy's head snapped up and looked wildly around until he finally focused on us.

"Maisie?"

He stumbled towards me and I grabbed hold of him before he fell. His usually spiky hair was flat and matted to his head. His face was streaked with dirt and blood and he was still in the uniform he'd been wearing when I'd spotted him at Warwick Castle but it was filthy, torn and bloody.

"Are you hurt?" I asked.

"It's not my blood." He pointed to the bodies lying on the ground next to the cart. Bile immediately rushed up my throat at the sight of a soldier with his insides outside his body.

Lizzie leant forwards and was sick on the ground. I looked away and swallowed hard, forcing the bile climbing up my throat back down again. The fog had lifted in places revealing bloodied grass and soldiers lying on the ground, their bodies twisted and disfigured. Some were moving, their groans overpowered by distant shouts of victory.

"Boy!" a man shouted from somewhere behind the cart. "I've got a live one."

Danny automatically started back towards the voice. I caught hold of his arm. "You're with us now."

We ran away from the battlefield and that man's voice. Although it was thinning I still felt protected by the fog. We only stopped when the battlefield noise had dulled to a murmur and we didn't have the energy to run any further.

Danny slumped on the ground. "I thought I was the only one," he said, rubbing his eyes.

"I saw you with the army in the castle. I was trying to shout after you..." I glanced at Lizzie.

"You do realise the ponies are in completely the opposite direction," Lizzie said still scowling at me. "Back towards that." She pointed vaguely in the direction we'd just run from.

I crouched next to Danny. "Did you realise what had happened at the castle when we time-shifted?"

He shrugged. "I don't remember much. I was told I'd hit my head. One of the soldiers found me unconscious by the castle wall and looked after me. It was only when I was marching with the army that I remembered that I'd left you down in the dungeon and then Nathan nicked my mobile. I remember chasing after him and shouting what an idiot he was when I fell to the ground."

Lizzie looked at me and raised an eyebrow.

Danny noticed and stood up. He nodded towards Lizzie. "How did you end up with her?"

"Everyone else had disappeared and, as far as I knew, so had you."

"You didn't think about dumping her at the first opportunity?" Danny asked.

Lizzie stepped towards him. "That's the thanks I get for walking and riding for days just to save you."

"I didn't need saving."

"Of course you didn't," Lizzie shouted, folding her arms across her chest. "You look like you have everything under control, covered in blood and crap."

"I've been in battle. I've watched soldiers die," he shouted, his voice cracking.

I pulled Lizzie away from Danny. "Just shut up both of you!"

A rumble sent a jolt up my legs. I fell to my knees as the ground shook and cracked beneath me. I reached out and grabbed Danny's hand: I didn't want to lose him again. Lizzie had fallen too – she said something but I couldn't hear over the rumble. She shouted again, "We're in the wrong place!"

Everything went black. The ground shuddered once more and then stilled. I thought I'd closed my eyes but then realised they were open and it was night. Still holding Danny's hand I stood up. I felt uncomfortably warm in my long-sleeved dress and woollen tights.

"This isn't 2012," I said.

"What's going on?" Danny said.

"We've time-shifted again," Lizzie said. "Robbie warned us there was a risk of time-shifting from Dunstable onwards."

Danny stepped closer to me. "Why's it dark?"

I shrugged. "If we can time-shift back centuries I guess it's not so strange to shift from day to night."

"We're in the same place right?" Lizzie said, squinting at the darkness.

"I guess so." There was still grass underfoot and I could make out a few trees against the night sky. "But it was so foggy before I doubt we'd be able to recognise where we are even if it was light."

"Well this is an adventure, isn't it," Danny said.

"Is that what you call this?" Lizzie said, her voice rising.

I stepped between them. "Seriously, we're going to get time-shifted again if you keep on arguing."

"Sorry," Danny said. "I only meant this beats our camping trip last summer."

Lizzie turned to me. "You're the boss. What do you suggest we do?"

"We should find out where we are. See if Barnet's back that way."

With Lizzie and Danny either side of me we walked back the way we thought we'd come. The air tasted different, sweeter somehow, and it was loads warmer even though it was night-time. We must have run for at least five minutes and we walked for at least twice as long before Danny stopped dead.

"This is the place of the battle." He waved his hand over the dark expanse of grass in front of us. Just as Warwick Castle had changed, so had the battle site – the soldiers' bodies, the fog and the sickly bitter smell that had choked us were all gone.

Lizzie put her hands on her hips. "How can you tell?"

"I had to scout it out the night before the battle."

"Okay fine," Lizzie said. "We're at the site of the Battle of Barnet but the battle's no longer here. So if it's not 1471 anymore, when is it?"

"Maybe we'll be able to find out in Barnet," I said.

Guided by the moonlight, we fought our way through the long grass until it was Lizzie's turn to stop dead. "We're so stupid. Robbie's map is in the saddlebags. Somewhere in the past."

I reached into the pouch on the belt of my dress and pulled out a folded piece of parchment. "This map?"

"What map?" Danny asked.

Lizzie glanced at me. Danny noticed and repeated, louder this time, "What map and who is Robbie?"

I handed him Robbie's drawing.

"We met someone who time-shifted in 2003 to the fifteenth-century but who managed to get back. He told us we needed to get to south London to have any chance of getting home. He's marked the spot with a cross."

"Are you serious? There's a way home?" Danny said, tracing his fingers over the map. "Why are we hanging about then?"

"Do you think there are people from the past walking around in our time?" Lizzie said, as we started walking again.

"Well, we've time travelled so anything's possible," Danny said. "But it's different, going back than forwards, not knowing what to expect. There are no surprises in the past."

Lizzie snorted. "You wanna bet?"

We reached the top of the slope and saw a cluster of houses spread out along the main road to London. Danny nudged me and pointed. On the horizon a small reddish glow lit up the night sky.

"What's that?" he said.

I squinted. "It looks like a massive bonfire."

Danny held up Robbie's map and traced his finger in that direction. "It has to be London."

Lizzie tugged the map from his hands and looked between it and the orangey red on the horizon. "As long as it's not the Great Fire of London."

Chapter Fifteen

We both stared at her.

"What?" she snapped, flinging the map at me. "I'm only joking."

"If that's the Great Fire of London..." I said slowly, "then it's 1666 and we've time-shifted forwards almost two hundred years."

Danny shook his head. "If that is the great fire and we have to get to the other side of London to get home, then we're in trouble."

"Point out the obvious why don't you," Lizzie said.

We fell silent and looked towards the red glow on the horizon.

"So what are we waiting for then?" I asked.

"Nothing," Danny said, and set off after me.

"Wait!" Lizzie's voice pierced the night. She remained rooted to the spot, with her hands on her hips and a face like a toddler who hadn't got their own way. "We have no food or water. The lighter, the money, the blankets Robbie gave us, everything is in the saddlebags back there," she said waving her arms about. "Back there in the past."

"Was she always this dramatic at school?" Danny asked me.

"Aaargh!" she screeched and stamped the ground with her feet. "I think I have every right to be 'dramatic' considering we're stuck in the past."

"Well," I said, "the sooner we start walking the closer we will be to getting home."

"Oh yeah, 'cause walking towards that," she said, pointing towards London, "isn't a death wish?"

"If you didn't love the sound of your voice so much we'd be in London already," Danny said and walked off.

"Why haven't we time-shifted again?" she snapped.

"What?"

"We're arguing so why aren't we being time-shifted?"

"Lizzie, we argued plenty of times when it was the two of us and we didn't go anywhere."

"We weren't on the line then. You know, the line Robbie drew down the map. The line goes right through Dunstable, St Albans, Barnet, all the way through the centre of London. He didn't want to go near Dunstable in case of being time-shifted again."

"I don't know, maybe it's all random," I said. "You said the riders in the wood shifted with no warning. Anyway, what does it matter if we time-shift again – as long as we're getting closer to our own time, it's all good."

"You're a freak, you know," she said, stomping past me, "enjoying this." She reached Danny at the top of the hill. "What are you looking at?"

"You," he replied as she disappeared down the

other side of the hill.

I sighed and forced my legs to walk up the hill to join Danny. Of all the people we could be stuck in the past with, it had to be Lizzie Andrews.

~

We picked our way by moonlight through scrubland towards Barnet. A church spire, dark against the sky, poked above the trees. Danny and me led while Lizzie sulked behind. There was so much I wanted to ask Danny but Lizzie's presence stopped me from saying anything to him. The grass thinned and suddenly we were back on the road we'd been following since Towcester. Barnet seemed bigger than the other towns we'd been through already yet it was eerily quiet. Timber-framed houses tightly packed both sides of the road and I noticed a cross chalked on one of the doors.

I stopped in the middle of the road, the quietness, almost deathliness of the place becoming clear. "I don't think we should hang around here," I whispered.

"We need to find somewhere sheltered to sleep," Lizzie said with a glare. "I'm not sleeping under a tree again."

I pointed to the door of the house we were closest to. "That house is marked with a cross to warn of the plague."

"You can stay here if you want, Lizzie," Danny said as he started walking faster along the road, "but I'm heading to London and finding food on the way."

I followed after him and smiled when I heard

Lizzie stomp after us. I wondered what was going on behind the cross-marked door. The suffering and slow, painful death caused by the plague. There was a whole chapter about it in our history book. We hadn't studied the Tudors or the Restoration period yet but I'd read ahead to the plague and the pus-filled boils the size of tennis balls beneath armpits.

We left Barnet and only stopped when the last house was out of sight. Danny, wide-eyed, stared at the road ahead that led to London.

"How long have you been awake for?" I asked.

He shrugged. "A while, I guess."

"So because Danny's tired you want to find somewhere to sleep now," Lizzie said.

"No, I'm just checking he's okay as an hour ago he was in the middle of a battle."

"I'm okay," he said. "And I want to keep moving. I want to try and get some new clothes." He lifted the edge of the grubby blood-stained tunic he'd been wearing since the castle.

"You do look a mess," I said and grinned at him.

Lizzie huffed. "Can we please at least just sit down for a few minutes and plan what we're going to do."

"Walk to London," Danny said.

"I know that," she replied, sitting down on the grass next to the road. I knew I was the one who had to keep the peace so I sat next to her and soon enough Danny joined me.

"What's there to talk about?" he asked.

"Lots," Lizzie said and glanced at me. "If we hadn't met Robbie we'd never have made it to Barnet on our own."

"We were doing okay," I said.

"But without Robbie we're on our own," Lizzie said. "And we need a story..."

"Like what?" Danny snorted. "Like hi, we're from the future, can we have some food...?"

"No," she said calmly. "The opposite. A believable story for why the three of us are wandering around on our own in the middle of the night and he looks like this." She pointed at Danny.

"Hey, if you'd done what I had to do..."

"You're arguing again," I cut in quickly. "How about we say our parents have died from the plague and we're heading to London to find family. How's that?"

"The plague bit might be a problem," Lizzie said. "We want people to feel sorry for us not freaked out."

"Okay," I said slowly, trying to rethink the idea. "Our parents have sent us to family in London for fear of the plague."

"I don't think it's very safe in London either," she said.

"One problem," Danny said. "I'm not dressed like I'm related to you two."

"Then you can be our servant," Lizzie said and stood up.

I grabbed Danny's arm. "Leave it. Don't waste your energy on her."

I pulled Danny to his feet. If it really was the Great Fire of London we were walking towards, I didn't think anyone would take much notice of us. At least I hoped that was the case as we set off again along the London road.

Chapter Sixteen

The sun finally appeared on the horizon and although I was carrying my cloak, I still felt hot in my dress. When we went up a hill we could see the reddish glow of the fire in the distance although it was less bright in daylight. And it was so quiet. There really wasn't another sound besides the birds singing in the trees and our footsteps. Even on our farm it was never this peaceful. There were always voices: Mum shouting across the yard to Ollie; Dad answering his mobile in the middle of the field; the rumble of the combine on a hot August day. Everyday life had always been filled with voices, music and artificial sounds... And now, nothing. I shivered.

"You okay?" Danny asked.

I nodded. "I was thinking about home."

"What do you think is happening back home?" he said. "Do you think they're still looking for us?"

I glanced between him and Lizzie. Lizzie was focused on the road ahead, her face set in a frown.

"We just disappeared," I said. "They're probably thinking the worst, that we've been abducted or..."

"Don't say it, Maisie," Danny said.

"Do you really think they're searching for us?" Lizzie asked.

"What do you think?" Danny said. "The three of us just disappeared in the middle of Warwick

Castle on a school trip in the middle of the day. There'll be a massive police search. We'd have made the national news and the front headlines of every newspaper. Except there will be no trace of us and no one will find us."

"It's not the fact that we'll be headline news that's bothering me, it's what our disappearance is doing to our families. If I'm thinking the only reasonable explanation for us disappearing is abduction, I hate to think what Mum, Dad and Ollie are thinking back home."

We trudged past farm labourers in a large field getting an early start on the harvest. I couldn't believe we were walking in what would eventually be the outskirts of twenty-first-century London and there wasn't a building in sight, although there must be a farm somewhere close by, maybe hidden by those trees across the other side of the field. I was conscious of the way we looked. Lizzie's and my dresses were authentic but for the fifteenth century and not the seventeenth. And Danny... the dried blood and dirt could be a problem. I guess we could always say he'd been in a fight. But why would anyone notice us? We were just kids after all and unless we did something to make people notice us then there was nothing to worry about. This was the adventure I'd always wanted so I was going to make the most of it. I knew Danny would feel the same. I reached out and squeezed his arm and he grinned at me.

"This is pretty mental," he whispered.

"A bit more of an adventure than our camping trip."

"It's rude to whisper," Lizzie said.

Danny caught my eye and raised an eyebrow. Again we fell silent and I concentrated on my feet pounding the ground. As the sun rose higher we began to pass people on the road. On our journey so far, apart from Robbie, we'd seen mainly peasants or traders but now there were fancy rich-looking people riding along the road. The open fields surrounding us began to be dotted with clusters of cottages. A huge white house, surrounded by trees and with rolling heathland in front, appeared in the distance.

Lizzie stopped dead, her mouth open. "I've totally been there."

"Really?" Danny said.

"It's an English Heritage place or something like that. I stayed with my aunt in London when I was filming *Harry Potter* and she made me go there. I wanted to go to the cinema."

There was a rumble behind us but before I had time to look, Danny pushed me and Lizzie off the road and into the grass verge as a carriage, pulled by four black horses, thundered past us towards London.

"Idiots!" Lizzie shouted after the carriage.

"They're in a hurry," I said, lifting the bottom of my dress out of the long damp grass.

"Maybe their house is on fire." Danny stepped back on the road.

"Serves them right," Lizzie said.

Danny turned to her. "Do you hate absolutely everyone?"

"No," she said and started walking, "just the people who annoy me."

"Isn't that everyone?" Danny muttered.

It wasn't much further until the fields gave way to cottages and then houses and a small town. The sky was a clear blue but in the direction the road headed it was fogged with smoke hanging over London. As we walked through the town I caught snippets of talk about the fire: "started in the King's bakers", "been burning since last night..."

History was happening and we were heading straight for it. We needed to be prepared before we got to London. We didn't need a cover story; we needed food, water and clean comfortable clothes for Danny. And most importantly Danny needed to sleep before we went any further.

"Hey look." I motioned towards a drinking fountain. I waited until Danny had gulped down some water. "I think we should stay here for the night."

"It's only like midday or something," Lizzie said.

"I know. But once we get to London we're not going to be able to sleep anywhere. It'll be too dangerous. And Danny, how long have you been awake for?"

He shrugged. "A long time."

Now he'd washed his face I could see how red and tired his eyes were. The town square was packed with people selling and bartering. A whiff of fresh bread floated from a bakery and made my mouth water and an inn stood across the other side of the square. "This town has everything we need," I said.

"Yeah," Lizzie said. "Only if we had money to buy stuff with."

I looked around. An old lady furiously bartered over a live chicken; a man sat in the gutter rocking back and forwards, begging for food. Then Lizzie's brooch caught my eye.

I pointed at it. "We don't need money, we can use that."

Without giving her time to protest I whipped the brooch off the front of her dress and placed it in her hands.

"We need food and a room so let's try the inn and see what we can get."

"It's your idea, you do this," she said, pushing the brooch back into my hands.

"Come on, Lizzie, you're the actress," Danny said, "improvise."

Lizzie faltered and glanced towards the inn. There was no way she'd be able to resist showing off and proving what a great actress she was after Danny's challenge.

"Fine," she said, plucking the brooch back out of my hand. "But let me do all the talking."

She took a deep breath, lifted the hem of her skirts and paced across the town square, dodging people, horses and animal dung. She stopped outside the inn and turned to Danny. "Act hurt,

like you're really in pain."
    She pushed the inn door open.

Chapter Seventeen

It was gloomy inside with the only light coming from two small dirt-ingrained windows and a large fireplace, which had a whole pig roasting on a spit, its fat dripping and fuelling the flames below. Lizzie walked to the bar leaving Danny and me hovering in the doorway. There was only one customer in the place – an old man slumped in the far corner, asleep or drunk or both, I couldn't tell.

The bar woman's face was red and glistened with sweat. Plump flesh spilled out of her too-tight corset. She dried a tankard with a cloth and looked at Lizzie but I couldn't hear what Lizzie asked her.

"Not without money you can't," the woman said, wiping the sweat from her forehead with the same cloth she'd used to wipe the tankard.

"That smells so good." Danny motioned towards the roasting pig.

"But please!" Lizzie said. "My friend was injured in a fight and he needs rest and some food."

"Is she actually crying?" Danny whispered.

The woman looked over at us and I nudged him. He winced and grabbed his chest and groaned. "Too much?" he asked.

I shook my head as the woman turned her attention back to Lizzie.

"I still need money for your board and keep even if he is hurt."

"I've got this," Lizzie said, unfolding her hand to reveal Robbie's brooch. The woman's eyes widened and she leant forward to examine it. "And where did you get that from?"

"It's a family heirloom," she sobbed and closed her fist around it again.

"Lizzie 'melodramatic' Andrews," Danny whispered.

I stifled a laugh as the woman drew herself upright. "I'm sure we can come to some sort of agreement..."

"This," Lizzie said, revealing the brooch again. "For lodging, food, clean clothes for my friend, as well as food to take with us when we leave."

The door behind us flew open and sent us stumbling further into the inn. Danny, still in character, let out a moan and slumped on the chair closest to him. A man was silhouetted in the doorway. He took off his hat and without a glance at us paced to the bar. His curly black wig fell about his shoulders and he flicked his long riding coat from beneath him before perching on a stool.

"The usual, Thomas?" the woman asked.

Lizzie had closed her fist again but the woman kept an eye on her as she poured the man his ale.

"There's talk all over of a fire in London," he said as she handed him the tankard.

"Well that's nothing new, Thomas."

"Oh this is different, Hannah," he said and took a long sip of his drink. "There's talk it was started deliberately at the King's bakers in Pudding Lane. It's destroyed the Old Swan and has reached as far as Stillyard already with no sign of it abating."

"Never," Hannah said, shaking her head.

"It's destroying everything in its path. Oliver's warehouse by all accounts is in danger if the wind doesn't change direction. All those barrels of brandy going up in flames. What a waste."

Hannah clicked her tongue and shook her head. "It's a bad enough business these days, what with the plague having torn us apart... and now this."

Lizzie coughed. "And what about our business?"

"Right, young lady," Hannah said wiping her hands down the front of her corset. "Let's get you sorted with rooms and some food." She held her hand open and Lizzie dropped the brooch into it. "Excuse me, Thomas," she said with a smile and a lowering of her heaving chest.

Lizzie turned and grinned at us. Danny raised his eyebrows. "She's going to be impossible now," he said, as we followed after her out of the heat of the inn to a gloomy back staircase.

"I need to take whatever business comes my way these days," Hannah said as we reached the top of the stairs. "Not many travellers around these parts since... well you know how it's been with the plague and all..."

Upstairs was dim and every floorboard creaked. The place felt empty unlike the fifteenth-century Dunstable inn.

"You can have these three rooms," she unhooked three keys from the bunch hanging around her waist. "There'll be roast pork later that you can eat downstairs." She looked at each of us again and Danny winced as her eyes reached him. She clicked her tongue and waddled off back down the hallway.

"Nice acting, Lizzie," Danny said before throwing his arm against his forehead. "Oh! My poor friend has been injured," he cried, doing a neat impression of her.

"Oh shut up," she said. "At least I got us somewhere to stay and food."

"He's only joking," I said as she frantically tried each of the keys in the nearest door.

"No I'm not," he said under his breath.

"I heard that," Lizzie said as the lock clicked and the door creaked open. She chucked the other two keys on the landing floorboards and slammed the bedroom door closed behind her. Danny laughed and picked the keys from off the floor and started trying them in the next door.

"There are numbers on the keys but none on the doors," he said.

I stared at the door Lizzie had shut herself behind and chewed my lip. "You shouldn't make fun of her."

"Why are you worrying about her?" Danny said as the second door swung open. "She wouldn't care about you."

"I know," I said, following him into the room.

"I just don't want to be as bad as she was to us at school."

"Is. As bad as she is."

"I've spent the last few days with her. She's better on her own."

"Yeah right..." Danny said and slumped on the bed. It creaked like a machine badly in need of oiling. "Ouch! This mattress is so scratchy."

"Life's pretty rough in the past," I said and smiled.

Danny sat up and crossed his legs. Dirt and blood were still ingrained on the side of his face, neck and arms. His clothes looked stiff with sweat.

"I didn't think I was going to see anyone again," he said, fiddling with the edge of his sleeve. "I don't know what I would have done if you hadn't found me."

"Did you have a plan?"

"Only to try and head back to Warwick if I was able to escape. I missed you. I miss Mum and my sisters so much." His voice cracked and he rubbed his eyes.

"Hey, Danny." I sat next to him on the bed and put my arm round his shoulders. "It'll be okay, I promise. We've had help from someone who's time-shifted back, we've got the map – look." I pulled Robbie's hand-drawn map out of my pouch. "X marks the spot."

"Yeah, yeah I know," he said, swinging his legs off the bed. "Thank you so much for finding me."

"You'd have done the same for me."

He went over to the small window and wiped his hand over the glass. I jumped off the bed and joined him, leaning on the window ledge. On the horizon the blue sky was grey and thick with smoke and seemed to cover a huge area.

"So this guy, Robbie, he's from our time?" Danny asked.

"Sort of. He was born in 1980, but in 2003 was time-shifted to the fifteenth century and then got shifted forwards in time to 1996, seven years before he'd first time-shifted."

"That sounds complicated."

"It is."

The smoke looked like a massive rain cloud hovering over London. Danny left the window and went to the chest of drawers and poured water from a jug into a bowl and washed his arms.

"Something else happened after Robbie left us," I said, watching him splash his face with water. "We were chased from the inn we were staying at by a man and woman on horses." Danny's hands stilled and he looked at me. "We hid in a wood but they found us; we ran but they caught Lizzie..."

"But..." he motioned to the room Lizzie was in.

"By the time I got back to her she was on her own. But the weirder thing was she said three other people, two women and a man, appeared from nowhere and fought off the two riders."

"Who were they?"

"We never found out. According to Lizzie they were trying to tell her something, but because she was screaming the whole time, she doesn't remember much."

"What does she remember?"

"It's pretty weird. The woman who spoke to her apparently looked like my older sister – if I had one. Oh and she called Lizzie by her name."

"Seriously?"

"Seriously."

"Couldn't they have found your names out from the inn?"

I shook my head. "We never told the innkeeper's wife our names and Robbie's letter just referred to us as his friends. And anyway, even if they knew our names how did they know Lizzie was Lizzie and not me?"

"So what else did Lizzie tell you?" he asked, scrubbing his neck with a chunk of soap.

"Just that they looked like they were in their twenties. Oh, and the man had a strange scar on the palm of one hand."

There was a plop as the soap dropped into the bowl. Danny swung round to face me, his eyes wide. "Maisie..." he said, stretching his right hand out towards me. The burn on the palm of his hand was the shape of a cross and bright red. "I burnt myself on the morning we left the castle. I stupidly tried to grab the horse brander by the wrong end. I barely touched it but it hurt so much."

"If this means what I think it does..." I grabbed his wrist and pulled him out into the hallway and banged on Lizzie's door. "Lizzie, let us in."

Silence.

"Leave it, Maisie," Danny said. "Why's it so important showing her?"

I banged on the door again.

"Go away!"

"Lizzie, it's important."

"Important enough to wake me?" she shouted. There was shuffling and then footsteps padded across the floorboards. The door clicked open and Lizzie appeared bleary eyed and frowning.

"I need to show you something." I pushed the door open with my foot and barged our way into the room.

"A little while ago, he," she said, stabbing a finger at Danny, "couldn't wait to get rid of me."

"Let's leave her to her tantrum, Maisie." Danny pulled his wrist from my grip.

"I'm not having a tantrum!" Lizzie screamed.

"Lizzie. Lizzie!" I grabbed her shoulders and shook her. "Just shut up for a second! Those three people who time-shifted in the wood... I think they might be us."

She stared at me with her hands on her hips. "I know."

"You know?" Danny said, barging past me.

"I don't *know*... what I mean is it doesn't surprise me that you think it's us."

"You're taking this way too calmly," I said.

She shrugged. "It crossed my mind but I thought it was a stupid idea. But then the more I thought about it... it's just the way that woman looked and spoke... I swear it could have been you, Maisie. I was trying to figure out why she let go of me just before they disappeared – it's like she knew she was going to time-shift."

"Why didn't you tell me all this before?"

"I pretty much thought you'd laugh at me."

"We're not laughing now," Danny said.

"Show her your hand."

He held out his right hand palm side up and Lizzie took a step back. "That's the same scar as the man had. Faded but the same."

The three of us looked at each other.

"This explains why everything felt familiar at Warwick Castle when we first time-shifted," I said. "It was fate. We were meant to travel back in time."

"What do we do now?" Lizzie asked.

"Exactly what we were planning on doing," I said. "Sleep, eat, then head for south London."

"I wish I'd listened to what she... you were trying to tell me."

"It doesn't matter, Lizzie, it's not going to affect our plan."

"Except," Danny said slowly. "Why are our grown-up selves wandering around in the past? Surely there's only one possible reason for that. We don't get home."

Chapter Eighteen

"**O**f course we're going to get home," I said.
Lizzie glanced between us. "For once he's actually got a point. Why else would we be time-shifting when we're older?"

"Just thinking about this is hurting my head," Danny said and handed me the remaining key. "For your room. I seriously need to sleep." He closed the door behind him.

"If we don't get home, Maisie..."

"It doesn't mean anything." I squeezed her arm. "Let's sleep and have some food. My mum always says things look better on a full stomach."

Lizzie raised an eyebrow. "Yeah, after a Sunday roast at home, maybe."

~

But I couldn't sleep. All I could think about was what had happened since we'd first time-shifted at Warwick Castle and what could happen as we walked closer to a burning London. If Lizzie was right and the woman who'd had hold of her in the wood was me... Did Lizzie not get a look at herself? How weird would that have been? She was right too – if we managed to get home, why would our older selves be trying to help us in the past? I propped myself up on the pillows and looked at the wooden floorboards and threadbare rug, the melted candles on the chest of drawers and the soot-filled fireplace. The bed was lumpy and filled with straw and felt well used; I wondered how many other travellers had slept on this bed. It was the first time I'd actually had the chance to stop and think – even at Robbie's there had been too much going on and so much to take in. Mum, Dad and Ollie would think they'd lost me forever. There would be no trace of us. One second we were there, the next second we were gone. Just like the people in the wood...

~

Thud, thud, thud...

I sat bolt upright, my neck aching from sleeping propped up on the pillows. My heart thumped as I looked around the dusky room and it took a moment to register... The inn on our way to London... 1666.

Thud. A fist on the door again. "Maisie, can I come in?"

My breathing slowed at the sound of Danny's voice.

"It's unlocked."

The door scraped open and Danny walked in holding a candle. He put the flame to the candles on the chest of drawers and warm light flickered across the room.

"Did you sleep?" I asked, rubbing my eyes. He was clean and dressed in new clothes.

"Do you like them?" He proudly pulled at the edge of breeches that reached his knees with stockings below. "Hannah found them for me; she said her nephew had grown out of them and the linen shirt. Also the roast pork will be served in a few minutes. It seriously smells good."

I swung my legs off the bed and padded to the window. The glow from the fire lit up the darkening sky. "It's getting bigger."

"That's why it's called the *great* fire."

"Ha ha," I said.

~

It was hot downstairs in the inn, despite the fire being reduced to glowing embers. There were a few more people than earlier sitting at the tables tucking into Hannah's roast pork. My stomach growled with hunger. Hannah waved us towards an empty table by one of the windows. Maybe if I closed my eyes I could believe I was in our local pub having Sunday lunch with Mum, Dad and Ollie.

"Maisie!" Danny snapped his fingers in my face. "You're daydreaming."

"Sorry."

"Have you got the map?"

I uncurled Robbie's hand-drawn map and laid it on the table. The three of us stared at it.

"We should plan our journey," Danny said.

"We could except we don't know where the fire is," I said.

Lizzie flattened out the creases in the map and tapped her finger on the line that crossed the River Thames from north to south London. "There's only one bridge so we have to head for it."

"It doesn't look that far once we get into London," Danny said.

"It's probably further than we think because Robbie's only drawn the main London roads." I skimmed my finger over the handwritten road names: Fleet Street, Cheapside, Thames Street, Pudding Lane. My finger stopped. "That's it, that's where the fire started. Pudding Lane – that's what the man talking to Hannah said earlier."

"Then it all depends on which way the wind is blowing," Danny said. He snatched the map off the table as Hannah bustled over with three plates of food and placed them in front of us.

"You scrubbed up nicely," she said, pinching Danny's cheek.

"Any news of the fire?" he asked.

She shook her head. "It's a bad business. They say it's spreading fast because of the hot summer and dry wind. I'm fearful for my sister, her husband and their boys. They're packing their belongings on to a cart ready to flee here if the wind changes direction... such a bad business."

"And which direction is the fire headed at the moment?" Danny asked.

"West so I've heard. It's destroyed the warehouses along the river. I hope you're not thinking of going near London?" She ruffled Danny's hair and we all shook our heads as she left us.

Our plates were piled high with chunks of roasted pork with carrots and potatoes smothered in melted butter.

"The crackling is amazing," Danny said, crunching through his mouthful.

Lizzie cut a ladylike portion of roast pork and popped it and a carrot into her mouth and chewed slowly. "Wow, this is like a proper roast dinner."

It was better. The meat was tasty and juicy and the vegetables were fresh and seasonal. My dad was an organic farmer and always wanted to convert everyone to eating organic. He would be proud of this meal. Without saying another word we finished every scrap of food on our plates and mopped up the juice with a chunk of wholewheat bread. To drink we had a tankard of weak ale each, which Danny downed in one. He leant back in his chair and patted his stomach. "That was the best meal I've ever had," he said.

I'd forgotten that less than twenty-four hours ago we'd found him blood-stained, bruised and starving in the middle of a battle and now it felt quite normal and homely in Hannah's inn. Danny leant across Lizzie and plucked a pack of cards from the windowsill behind her.

"Fancy a game?" He shuffled the cards and began dishing them out face down in front of us.

"I don't know any card games," Lizzie said.

"This one's easy." Danny placed the last card down. "Even for you."

Lizzie's nostrils flared but she kept her mouth shut.

~

I didn't want to break this moment of relative normality – even Danny and Lizzie looked quite happy in each other's company – but I couldn't relax with the thought of the fire getting bigger every second we spent here.

"If the fire's spreading west we're in trouble," I said as Danny gathered the cards together. "The bridge might be cut off already."

"Well there's only one way to find out," Danny said, scraping his chair back.

Lizzie frowned. "What's the rush?"

"The possibility of getting home, that's what," I said.

"Let's get packed," Danny said.

Lizzie raised her hands and pointed at herself. "I'm wearing everything I've got."

"Me too."

"Wait here a minute," Danny said, before winding his way between the tables.

I tapped the cards into a neat pile and placed them back on the windowsill.

Lizzie scowled and peered out of the window at the darkness. It was too hot and stuffy inside and all the food and ale was making me sleepy. I told myself that it would be good to walk it off. The inn was full with people eating and drinking. The men were dressed in plain clothes and the women in earthy coloured dresses. Me and Lizzie stood out in my pale green and her gold dress. But no one seemed to take any notice of us; the main topic of conversation was the fire.

Danny reappeared with a lit lantern in one hand and a sack in the other, which he dumped on the table. "Hannah gave us food for our journey. Pork, cheese and bread."

"Why are we travelling at night?" Lizzie asked, her voice beginning to whine again.

"What difference does it make?" Danny asked.

"I just don't think it's such a good idea

travelling at night."

"Why not?" Danny swung the sack over his shoulder and handed me the lantern.

"Because it's dark, it's quiet, it's dangerous..."

"London's on fire," I said. "It's not going to be dark or quiet."

"Just dangerous," Danny said with a grin.

We walked to the inn door and suddenly, despite the stifling heat, I didn't want to leave the safety and comfort of the inn. I glanced back to where a hot-faced Hannah poured ale into pitchers for thirsty customers. "You be careful out there," she called.

I nodded and waved before following Lizzie and Danny outside and shutting the inn door firmly behind me. It was a warm sticky night and it would have been darkest black except for the red glow on the horizon and the flickering light from our lantern. The town square was empty of its traders, townspeople and animals. There was no going back now. We were headed for the Great Fire of London.

Chapter Nineteen

"What else have you got in that bag?" Lizzie asked. "Did she give you any money?"

He shook his head. "But we've got food."

Lizzie huffed. "I bet that brooch was worth loads more than we got for it."

We rejoined the London road on the other side of the town square. We passed the water fountain we'd stopped at earlier and I couldn't believe it was still the same day. After shifting from one century to another, it didn't really matter whether it was day or night any longer. Time was meaningless. I walked between Lizzie and Danny and held the lantern out in front of us to light our way, not that we could go wrong with London burning so brightly ahead of us. What I was worried about was what we'd find when we got there. If I hadn't been so scared of those riders and if Lizzie had listened to the woman who had saved her instead of screaming we might have found something out. If those three people were us, if they really were stuck in the past, then I figured what they'd wanted to tell us was pretty important.

Our shoes scuffed the road and the lantern squeaked as it swung from side to side as we walked. Lizzie hummed.

"Do you have to make that noise?" Danny asked.

"The silence is freaking me out," she replied and started humming again.

"Humming some rubbishy boy band song is not going to make you any safer. It might draw all the creepy people and murderers to us."

"Why do you have to say stuff like that?" she said, and stopped humming.

I liked the quietness – it reminded me of our farm at night. Being a few miles from Hay-on-Wye, our nearest neighbour's window was only a speck of light in the distance. With no city glow, on a clear night the black sky would be littered with stars. But there was always the occasional sound of a car passing by at the end of our lane. Here there was nothing.

Danny shifted the sack on to his other shoulder and I switched the lantern into my other hand. There was a gentle rumble of cartwheels in the distance. We all stopped.

"Where's that coming from?" Danny asked. "Behind us?"

"Not sure," I said. "Let's wait for it to pass."

The grass at the side of the road was long and there weren't any trees to hide behind so we stood and listened as the rumble grew louder.

"Blow the candle out," Lizzie hissed.

"We've got no way of lighting it again if I do." I placed the lantern in front of us on the edge of the road. "The sky's lit up like bonfire night so we'll be seen anyway."

A horse and cart appeared out of the darkness from the direction we'd just come. Two lanterns attached to the front of the cart lit up a shadowy figure holding the reins. The horse plodded along and it was the squeaky cartwheels that made such a noise on the uneven road.

"Whoa!" the man on the cart shouted and the horse halted in front of us. Lizzie backed further into the grass.

The man's face was cast in shadow.

"Bit young to be out wandering on your own," he grunted before spitting over the side of the cart on to the road.

"Yuck," Lizzie said under her breath.

My heart thudded in my throat. We'd safely made it this far and now we were about to be done in by some lone psycho man before we'd even reached London.

"We're on an errand that's all," I said trying to control the wobble in my voice. "To our aunt's in London... to help out because of the fire."

"Is the fire as bad as they say it is?" the man asked. His voice sounded like he'd eaten gravel.

"Um, we don't know," I said. "We've not got there yet." I stared at him not knowing what to do or if I should say anything else. His cart was empty and his horse, with its drooping ears and matted mane, looked old and tired. He erupted into a hacking cough and spat out whatever he'd brought up.

Danny stepped forwards and picked up the lantern from the edge of the road. "We'll be on our way then," he said, hooking his free arm in mine. "Come on, Lizzie."

The man grunted and flicked the reins and the horse began to move. We walked along the edge of the road until the horse had picked up the pace enough for the cart to pass us.

"Aaargh!" Lizzie yelled as soon as the horse and cart were out of sight. "He freaked me out. This is stupid walking at night. Anything could have happened."

"But it didn't," I said, although I didn't have as much confidence as when we'd first left Hannah's inn.

"But it could have done," Lizzie mumbled before stalking off. "Let's please just get to London."

~

The closer we got to London, the more people we saw and we didn't bother to huddle at the side of the road. My grandma always told me the best form of protection was walking with confidence so that's what I tried to do: shoulders back, head up, purposeful walk. There were a few people heading away from London, a lucky few with clothes and their belongings piled on to a horse and cart; the unlucky ones, like a family with three young children, struggled to carry what they could.

Houses began to clutter the edge of the road, spreading out in rows towards the direction of the fire. Even though it was the middle of the night there were plenty of people about. Two women leant out of their top windows shouting across the road to each other. I noticed a difference in the air – the fresh and strong farmyard smells of animals and drying hay had given way to something a lot more potent and unpleasant like rotting vegetables mixed with wee. The smell caught in the back of my throat and made me gag and we were still only in the outskirts of London.

The houses became more tightly packed the further we walked. Lanes veered off on either side of the main London road where the sticky-out upper storeys and roofs of the houses hanging over the lane nearly touched each other. The sky was lit up so brightly by the fire it felt like a weird sort of sunset rather than the middle of the night. I couldn't believe anyone would be asleep in the city while the fire raged; they'd be too scared that the wind would change direction and chase the flames towards them. Because we were walking through the outskirts of London now and not on higher ground we couldn't see the flames, just a smoky redness clouding the sky. I smelt burning wood mixed with something stronger and bitter and it looked like the smoke was being blown this way.

Up ahead a crowd of people gathered in the street, shouting, talking and jostling each other. Horses stomped and babies wailed. There were people near uniformed guards at a stone gatehouse, waving their fists at each other.

"No one said there were guarded gates to get into London," Lizzie said.

I pulled the map out and for the first time saw the black line around the centre of London. "It must be the city wall. Maybe it wasn't guarded when Robbie drew it in 1471."

Danny nudged me. "Look who it is," he said. Towards the side of the road away from the crowd by the city gates, the old man and his horse and cart were in a more orderly queue of people waiting to talk to the guards. "Come on!"

We ran after Danny and joined the back of the queue behind a sobbing woman holding a snotty nosed baby on her shoulder.

"Why do you think they're questioning everyone?" Lizzie whispered.

I shrugged. "I don't know but it looks like people are being let out of London without a problem."

The baby's eyes were red and puffy and oozed pus. He sneezed and all three of us took a step back, while his mother hushed him by rocking from side to side.

It was the old man's turn to step up to the gate.

"What's your business in London?" the guard asked him.

"I'm offering my services," he said, pointing over his shoulder to his empty cart, "to the poor people of London."

"And how much will you be charging the 'poor people of London'?"

"A fair price for the trouble and danger I'll be putting myself in."

The guard looked him up and down and glanced at the empty cart.

"No one's allowed into London tonight. King's orders. Come back at dawn."

I thought the old man was going to argue but with a glance at the guard's sword, he pulled at the horse's reins and trundled the wagon over to the other side of the road.

"We have no chance," Danny whispered.

The guard stepped forward and addressed the line of people. "No one's to be let in tonight! On the King's orders. You can all stay at Hatton Garden for the remainder of the night."

The people in front and the few who'd joined the queue behind us grumbled before beginning to drift away.

"I guess we follow them," I said.

We left the old man muttering to himself by the edge of the road and followed the woman and her sickly baby down winding cobbled lanes past houses, an inn and a big open market place. We crossed a bridge over a narrow river to a wide road called Holborn Hill with large houses lining each side.

"How much further is it?" Lizzie said when we turned right on to a cobbled road called Field Lane with tightly packed houses on both sides.

"Stop moaning," Danny said.

The Hatton place was a huge square field surrounded by large houses and gardens. What stopped all three of us in our tracks was the mass of people camped out on every available space. It looked like the whole of London had been made homeless. Families slept among their belongings, dogs wandered about and horses, tied to wagons, grazed. We picked our way through the makeshift camps set up on the field, avoiding staring at people squatting down and pissing into pots until we found a bare patch of grass.

"We so should have stayed at the inn," Lizzie said, flopping down on the ground. "What's the point of being here if we can't get into London."

"It's not that we can't get into London," Danny said, "it's just we can't get in tonight."

I wanted to be back at the inn too. The ground was bum-numbingly hard, the earth cracked and the grass shrivelled. Most people were asleep or trying to sleep; those near us were lying on their belongings or if they were lucky on the back of a cart. It was surprisingly quiet apart from a couple of babies crying and the occasional snort from a horse or someone coughing.

"What about the plague?" Lizzie whispered.

"What about it?" I bundled up my cloak into a pillow shape.

"What if these people have the plague?"

"Lizzie," Danny said. "If you really did see our future selves then you know we're not going to die tonight from the plague."

"Okay, fine. But what are so many people doing here?"

"You can be so stupid at times," Danny said, curling himself up into a ball and resting his head on his hands. "Look around properly. Everyone here must have lost their homes in the fire."

Lizzie glanced around, huffed and then lay down on her cloak. I blew out the flame in the lantern and lay on my side with my head resting on my cloak. I gazed up at the flaming red and orange glow spread across the night sky. The field and people were bathed in blood red. With every breath I could taste smoke and we were nowhere near the fire yet. Somewhere close by a baby screamed.

"Shut that child up," a gruff woman's voice snapped.

I curled myself tighter into a ball and wondered what would happen if the baby didn't stop crying. I watched the dark figures of newly arriving people highlighted against the red sky as they worked their way across the field. The inn seemed a long way off; Robbie, little more than a distant memory and home... Home felt like a dream.

Chapter Twenty

I didn't get a lot of sleep as the smoke tickled my throat so much that I kept waking up coughing. Every part of me ached from sleeping on the dry ground. This was more uncomfortable than sleeping on the floor of a straw-filled room or beneath the tree in the wood near Warwick.

"Bring back the tent," Lizzie moaned as she struggled to sit up. "Stupid crying babies."

"As caring as ever," Danny said from where he lay on the ground, his hands tucked beneath his head. "I slept great."

"Oh, I forgot you both like roughing it."

"I thought we'd agreed we were going to stop arguing in case we time-shift again." I shook the dried bits of grass off my cloak and folded it up.

"Yeah 'cos time-shifting again couldn't be worse than our present situation."

"Fine, Lizzie, if you don't get the importance of reaching the other side of the river as soon as possible then can we at least be nice to each other? Please?"

"As long as he is too."

"Danny?" I asked.

He nodded, rolled on to his side and curled himself up into a ball.

"Satisfied?" I asked Lizzie.

"For the moment." She stood up and stretched.

"There are so many people here."

The field was surrounded by three-storey timber houses and was filled with people and their belongings. People must have continued to arrive throughout the night because there was barely a patch of green left. The family camped nearest us had bedding and pillows and their three scrawny kids were still asleep, curled up together under a blanket. The mother was sorting through the rest of their belongings salvaged from their home: plates and cups, spoons, cooking pots, clothes and candles. Their whole life was here. Lizzie had wandered off to the edge of the field and stood with her arms folded looking towards London. It was the second morning since the fire had started and it was burning worse than ever. The sky was either red from the flames or black from the smoke that choked the sky overhead. If all the people camped out here had fled London then the fire must have spread far already. The longer we spent here the worse it was going to be and we still had to get past the guards at the city gates.

I gently shook Danny's shoulder. "Are you okay to get going?"

He moaned and struggled to his feet. "Can't we leave her here?" He nodded towards Lizzie.

"Just ignore her, Danny."

"That's virtually impossible; her voice is so whiny. She's so full of herself."

I put the lantern in the sack and picked it up.

"I'll carry it," he said, taking it from me and

swinging it over his shoulder. "Let's go get her then."

We set off across the field, stepping over sleeping people sprawled on the ground and avoiding wooden chests, cooking pots and animals. With each breath I took, I gathered a lungful of smoke that nearly made me gag. Danny walked right past Lizzie and headed for Field Lane. I tapped her on the shoulder. "We're going to try and get into London."

She nodded and we trailed after Danny.

"What were you thinking about?" I asked.

"What I'll miss if we don't get back."

"You can't think like that."

"I'm just being realistic." She tucked a loose hair behind her ear. "I mean the fact our older selves are wandering through time says as much."

"So, what would you miss?"

She frowned at me. "Not a depressing subject to talk about at all."

"Tell me. I'm interested that's all."

"My family, obviously. I already miss my clothes, my GHDs and my mobile. Imagine never doing normal things again like going to the cinema, eating Christmas dinner or even going to school? I miss my boyfriend too," she said with a sideways glance at me.

"I didn't know you had a boyfriend."

"You don't know him. I met him on holiday in Portugal but he lives in Cardiff."

"You kept that quiet."

"My friends know about him. Me and you don't

exactly hang out together."

"Hurry up!" Danny shouted from the end of the lane. We jogged over Holborn Bridge, following Danny as he weaved his way past carts and people working their way towards the gate into London. We caught up with Danny when he stopped next to a church called St Botolph's that we'd passed last night.

Aldersgate Street resembled a car park for horses and carts. People and their animals – plump ponies and scrawny dogs – filled every part of it from London gate backing right up the street.

"They don't seem to be letting anyone into London yet," Danny said. "But there are masses of people being let out."

"Do you think they will let us through?" Lizzie asked.

"I was thinking," Danny said, "that we might have a better chance of being let in if we had a proper reason for needing to go to London."

"We're going to find family, isn't that a good enough reason?" Lizzie said.

"Maybe not when most people are trying to leave. But if we were going into London to help people escape..."

"I don't get it," Lizzie said, crossing her arms.

"That old guy we met on the road last night, he's over there asleep on his cart. He said to the guard he was going to London to help people move their belongings from their houses. That's our way in. All we need to do is persuade him that with us he can earn more money because we can help him load his cart quicker. What do you think?"

"It's worth a try," I said.

"I'll go talk to him."

"Great," Lizzie said with a flick of her hair. "Now we're going to have to work our way through London."

"As long as it means we get through those gates then we're a bit closer to home," I said.

Lizzie folded her arms across her chest and frowned. There was no way she'd be convinced that an idea of Danny's would be a good one. We stayed in the shadow of the church while Danny weaved his way across the crowded street. He avoided a snarling dog and I lost sight of him, but he was soon in front of the cart and tapping the sleeping man on his shoulder.

"The old guy's probably dead," Lizzie said after he didn't look like he was waking up.

"You can't say that."

"I just did. Didn't you hear him coughing his guts up last night?"

"I did but that doesn't mean he's dead now." Danny had both his hands on the old man's shoulders and was shaking him. He suddenly sat upright and sent Danny stumbling backwards. "See."

"With lungs like his he's not going to last long breathing in smoke in London."

"Do you have to be so dramatic?"

It looked like Danny was doing all the talking but we were too far away to see if the man looked

154

angry or interested. Danny turned round and put his thumbs up at us.

"Come on," I said, grabbing Lizzie's arm with one hand and hitching my dress up with the other. We dodged horse dung as we elbowed our way past people.

The old man grunted some kind of greeting when we reached him.

"Nice one, Danny," I said under my breath.

The man looked sharply at me. "And you don't want no payment or reward like the boy says for helping me?"

I shook my head. "No, sir, we just want to get into London."

He eyed each of us up, spat green phlegm on to the ground by our feet and pointed to the cart. "Get in there and keep your mouths shut."

We did as we were told and clambered up the side of the wooden cart and sat on the dusty floor.

"Great," Lizzie whispered. "More hanging about."

"You never stop moaning," Danny said. "You're fed up when we're walking, you don't want to wait for anything, you don't like..."

"Can you both just stop arguing for five minutes?"

We sat in silence and watched the hazy sun rise higher in the sky until it was masked by smoke. At the gate the first person from outside London was let in and a ripple of excited chatter went through the waiting crowd like a wave. Even the old man sat up straight and took hold of the reins in anticipation. We didn't move for ages and the waiting crowd's excitement changed to frustration, then anger and shouts. A scuffle broke out at the gate but we couldn't really see anything, only heard a cry as someone fell to the ground. Then suddenly there was movement and wheels began to creak and conversations died down as the crowd shuffled forward.

The old man flicked the tired horse with the reins and, barely raising its head, the poor horse crept forward as fast as the people and animals in front would allow. Danny got to his knees, rested his elbows on the edge of the cart and leant over to see what was happening at the gate.

"They're not letting everyone through," he said.

"Shut it," the old man snapped. "I told you to be quiet."

Danny sat back down in the cart and raised an eyebrow at me. Lizzie scowled at him but I don't think he noticed.

Despite the hard slats of wood rubbing against my back, I was nodding off by the time the cart halted and the guard asked, "What's your business in London?"

"As I stated last night," the old man said, "I'm offering my services to the people of London in their time of need."

The guard snorted. "And the children?"

"They're helping me." The old man grinned a toothless grin.

"They're yours?" the guard asked with raised

eyebrows.

"My sister's bastards. They're helping me," he repeated. "For King and country and all."

"What does he mean, 'bastards'?" Lizzie said.

"Shush," Danny and I both said as the old man glared at her.

I held my breath as the guard looked at each of us before focusing his attention back on the old man. "On you go," he said. I breathed again, the horse plodded forwards, the wheels creaked and we finally entered London.

Chapter Twenty-One

On the other side of the gate the houses were even more squashed together making the wide road claustrophobic. It was packed with people, carts and horses jostling each other for space while hurrying in both directions in and out of London. The air was hot and heavy with heat and smoke that caught in the back of my throat. The old man started his hacking cough again.

We held on tight to the sides of the cart as we rumbled down the road and I stopped leaning over the side when a man carrying a boy on his shoulders knocked into me. Some of the people we passed had flushed, soot-ingrained faces and a couple of the women were crying. The smoke-filled sky above was almost blocked out by the roofs nearly touching. We passed an ironmonger and a bakery tucked between houses. I suddenly realised I was hungry and we'd gone without breakfast. I thought about asking Danny what food we had left in our sack but he was peering over the edge of the cart taking everything in, the same as Lizzie was doing on the other side.

The smell, a really horrible mixture of wee, poo, rotting vegetables and smoke, got worse the further down the road we went. So did the noise and heat and I wiped sweat off my face with the sleeve of my dress. We reached a crossroads jammed with people, and the old man steered the horse and cart to the left through the mob and on to a wider street called Cheapside. Other horses and carts rammed into the side of ours and I was glad when the road opened up and the crowds eased a little. On the right was a huge church; its square bell tower disappeared into the black smog above.

"What church is that?" I shouted to the old man.

"St Paul's," he grunted.

"As in St Paul's Cathedral? *The* St Paul's?" I asked.

"I've been to St Paul's and it doesn't look anything like it," Lizzie said.

"That's because it's probably going to burn to the ground and they'll have to rebuild it," Danny said.

"And you know this because?"

"Because I'm guessing that's what happens."

Hot wind buffered my face and embers from the fire whipped up by the wind settled on our clothes and in our hair. We passed coffee houses and another church. People dragged their belongings out of their houses and into the street. A tavern called The Bull Head was still open and men stood outside with tankards in their hands. The snippets of conversations I caught were all about the fire. The old man turned the horse and cart sharply to the right into Bow Lane, which was full of large and grand-looking houses still tightly packed together. It felt hotter and the noise of people shouting and screaming got louder. We turned left into another street at the bottom of the lane and suddenly there was the fire. It was much further down the road but flames ate away at the houses on both sides, leaping into the sky alongside plumes of black smoke. Smoke clouds masked the midday sun and the sky itself looked on fire.

The old man's slumped shoulders suddenly straightened. Sweat poured down my face. My heavy dress stuck to my skin. I leant towards Danny. "We should get off as soon as he decides to stop."

Lizzie crawled across the cart and sat next to us. "Aren't we getting a bit too close?" Her face was bright red and shiny. I imagined that this was what it would be like to sit in a sauna, minus the sound of splintering wood and flames roaring as they engulfed a building.

"Whoa there!" the old man shouted, tugging on the reins until the poor horse stumbled to a halt. "Madam, do you require any help?" he asked, putting on an unconvincing posh voice.

We scrambled to our feet and peered over the cart at a well-dressed and very pregnant woman standing among her belongings outside a large three-storey house, which was definitely in the fire's path.

"My husband was called away to Whitehall and our servant was making his way with our horses and carriage from Bishopsgate but has sent word the fire has cut him off," she said with tears streaming down her face. "Everything will be lost by the time he makes it through." She clutched her hands to her swollen stomach.

"We'll help you," Danny said, getting ready to jump from the cart.

The old man's arm shot across Danny's chest. "Not so fast, boy." He turned to the woman. "We'll help you all right but I need payment."

The woman nodded. "Anything, whatever you want, my husband will reward you handsomely. Just help us, please."

The old man spat on the ground. The fire was spreading fast and I could see the heat haze shimmering above the smoking chimney pots.

"Those candlesticks," he said gruffly, pointing to some of her belongings on the front step. "They gold?"

She nodded.

"I'll take them as down payment." He held his hands out and with great difficulty the woman leant down to pick them up and handed them to him.

"He's unbelievable." I started to climb over the cart.

"Wait... wait," Lizzie said grabbing my arm. "We're not actually helping are we?"

"Her house is about to burn down," Danny said.

"Exactly. Shouldn't we be heading away from the fire not into it?"

"Not if we want to cross the Thames by the bridge." I took the crumpled map from the pouch around my waist and pointed to the line crossing the wide river. "If we're lucky we might be able to reach it by walking along Thames Street."

"Oi!" the old man snapped. He wrapped the gold candlesticks in a ragged piece of cloth and tucked them beneath his seat at the front of the cart. "I didn't help you get into London just to do nothing. Get to work!"

We clambered over the side of the cart and jumped down on to the cobbles. The street heaved with people pushing past each other and carts being wheeled by hand towards the fire. Horses were loaded with belongings and people shouted between houses further down the street warning of the fire's advance.

"Get what she wants from inside," the old man said gruffly. "And no pocketing anything."

"We're not scavengers like..." I pulled Lizzie away from him before he heard and left him putting the lady's belongings already out on the street into his cart.

"I need the chest from the hallway and the silverware from the dining room," the lady told Danny. "And my husband's paperwork from his study on the first floor."

She looked scarily pale; her face, throat and skin above her bodice were soaked with sweat. Up close I could see how young she really was, not much older than my eighteen-year-old cousin.

"Don't worry," I said. "We'll get everything for you."

She gripped my arm really tightly. "My dog, he's upstairs. Please, you have to get my dog for me."

"I'll find your dog."

"Thank you," she said as tears mingled with the sweat on her face. "He's called Charlie."

I followed Lizzie and Danny into the house. After the brightness of the day, it was gloomy and stuffy inside. Danny headed straight for the large chest against the entrance hall wall.

"Grab the other end, Maisie," he said.

"I have to find her dog. Lizzie, help Danny." I clattered up the stairs before they had a chance to argue.

The first-floor landing was a little brighter with smoky daylight streaming through a window overlooking the street. Apart from one door that opened on to a large panelled room with a writing desk in front of the window, all the other doors off the landing were closed. I began to climb the stairs to the top floor when I heard a bark.

"Charlie?" I ran to the top landing and pushed open the doors of each bedroom until I saw the most gorgeous King Charles spaniel, barking his head off in the middle of a four-poster bed hung with gold drapes. He saw me and abruptly stopped barking and let out a whine.

"Hey Charlie, what are you doing up here on your own?" His tail wagged and he waddled over to the edge of the bed. He was a white and tan colour and so soft with huge floppy ears and big brown eyes. I scooped him into my arms and his wagging tail flicked back and forwards into my face. "Come on, let's get out of here before the whole place burns down."

I was about to walk out of the door when a thud on the floorboards behind me made me stop.

"Maisie, wait!"

Chapter Twenty-Two

After spending so much time with her I would have recognised Lizzie's voice anywhere. But the Lizzie standing next to the four-poster bed was all grown-up and gorgeous. She'd always been the pretty and popular girl in school but now her long blonde hair looked even blonder and sleeker, her skin was lightly tanned and her blue eyes and pink full lips made her look like a model. She wore a black short-sleeved top which revealed a hint of a tattoo at the top of her arm and black skin-tight trousers that showed off a figure that the Lizzie I knew would die for. She had a large silver locket on a chain around her neck and a chunky watch with a black strap on her wrist.

"Hello, Maisie," she said, stepping forward.

I closed my mouth. Charlie growled at her.

"I thought I'd find you up here."

"So you're future Lizzie. We were right about you."

She laughed. I don't think I'd ever heard Lizzie laugh before. She sat on the edge of the bed and patted the bedcover next to her. "Sit here and let me explain."

I pointed to the stairs behind me. "Shouldn't we be getting out of here?"

She shook her head. "There's time. I have a hissy fit because of what happens when you get down there with that dog, so a little while longer won't matter."

I'd been in some bizarre situations since we first time-shifted but this was probably the strangest. I was having a civil conversation with Lizzie "the bully" Andrews in a seventeenth-century house about to be burnt to the ground by the Great Fire of London. Except this wasn't the Lizzie I knew – she was downstairs lugging furniture out of the house while almost certainly arguing with Danny. My head hurt from the craziness of it all but I wanted answers. Stroking Charlie's soft ears I stepped back into the room.

"How old are you?" I asked.

"Twenty-six."

I worked the numbers out in my head. "Fourteen years? You've been time-shifting for fourteen years?"

"Don't freak out, Maisie," she said, patting the bed again. "And sit down before you drop that ridiculous dog."

"He's a King Charles spaniel and he's gorgeous," I said with a smile as a hint of the Lizzie I recognised appeared before me. I sat next to her on the springy bed and although it was rude I couldn't help but stare at her. "Where are the others? You know, Danny and me? We're okay right?"

"Of course, you're both fine. We decided it would be best if I came on my own as all three of us might be a bit much and trust me, coming face to face with yourself whether older or younger is a totally freaky experience."

"Lizzie was hysterical when you turned up in the woods."

"She didn't even see me and she was a wreck. We should have talked to you but you weren't the one who needed saving. I forgot how hot-headed and irrational I used to be."

"So what were you trying to tell her?"

"We were there for three reasons. Firstly to save you from those people, secondly to explain who we were and thirdly to warn you not to trust anyone."

"No one at all? What about Robbie? He helped us, he probably saved our lives."

"Robbie's a good guy but there are others out there who shouldn't be trusted so it's best to trust no one."

"Why should we trust you?"

She shot me a look identical to the one Lizzie downstairs would have given me. "You're kidding right? That's like saying you don't trust yourself." She tucked a loose hair behind her ear. "Me, you and Danny want the same thing. We want to get home. The only difference for us, fourteen years in the future, is it's too late. We're not children anymore. We could go back to that moment in Warwick Castle when we first time-shifted if we wanted to, but that'd take some explaining. But if we'd done things differently, if we'd not followed Robbie's map then we'd have had the chance of going home."

"Robbie's map is wrong?"

"Not by much but trust me that made all the

difference."

Charlie was heavy in my arms and I shuffled him into a more comfortable position. "Wait a second, I thought you said we could trust Robbie?"

"You can, he's just a little misguided. May I?" she asked, reaching into the pouch around my waist for the map.

"How did you know the map was there?"

She shot me another "Lizzie" look and I bit my lip. She spread the hand-drawn map out on the bed between us.

"See." She pointed to Robbie's X on the map just south of the Thames. "He's miscalculated. Time-shifting from that spot takes you to the future."

"But we want to go to the future."

She shook her head. "You want to go to the present, which is 2012."

"So what are we supposed to do?"

Future Lizzie took a pen from the bag slung across her chest. She drew a larger X on the map further south from the Thames than Robbie's black one. "This spot is the place you'll all end up getting home. Now, in 1666 that exact spot is a small cottage that we own – one of our safe houses." She drew a cottage next to the X. "You won't miss it if you follow the main road from London Bridge and after you walk through Southwark the next hamlet you reach has an old oak tree in the middle of the road and the cottage is down a track on the left. It has an apple tree and a well out the front. There's a rucksack of supplies in the bedroom."

I shook my head trying to take it all in. I had so many questions. "I don't get it. If this spot here," I said pointing at the new X, "gets us home, why do we need supplies?"

"Because there's a snag. You may have noticed when we first time-shifted we ended up in Warwick Castle in 1471. At the Battle of Barnet you were time-shifted to 1666 to the spot where the battle had taken place nearly 200 years before."

"So," I said slowly, "that means if we time-shift from this cottage on the other side of the river we'll end up in the same place in 2012."

"Exactly, except in 2012 that same spot will be someone's back garden in a street in Southwark. Then you need to get back to Warwick Castle as quickly and safely as you can. In the rucksack are twenty-first-century clothes for you to change into. Walking round London dressed like you are now is going to draw even more attention to yourselves than three thirteen-year-olds out and about on their own on a school day."

"I'm twelve," I said.

"Anyway, you'll find Tube tickets from Borough station to Victoria and from there you'll have train tickets to Warwick. There's also money, food, drinks, a London A-Z and a map of Warwick."

"You're talking like these supplies are already there."

"They are. We were going to give you the

rucksack in the wood but it was safer to get those riders away from you."

I sat in silence and stroked Charlie's floppy ears. My head felt like it was going to explode with all the information. Time had become meaningless. "The people chasing us in the wood, who were they?"

She played with the locket on her necklace. "They're from the future."

"Like the future, future?"

"Like the twenty-second century."

"But why are they after us?"

"I've explained too much for now. We're looking out for you, that's all you need to know," she said and folded the map and popped it back into my pouch. "Think of it like this: time isn't one straight never-ending line heading into the distance. Remember, we're time shifters, we have the ability to jump from one period of time to another as we choose. There are millions of variations and pinpointing ourselves at certain points or a place in time has not been easy."

"So how do we time-shift? I mean when we get to this cottage how do we time-shift back to 2012? By starting an argument?"

Future Lizzie laughed. "That might work. Arguing always seemed to help in the beginning and with me there you shouldn't have much trouble. Any conflict or trauma seems to be the initial cause of a shift. But there is another way: with enough belief and focus on the period in time you want to reach you can make yourself time-shift. How do you think I got here today?"

"That's impossible."

"No it's not. It took us long enough to figure it out but it's not impossible because you were the one to discover it."

"Me?"

"Believe in yourself, Maisie. You have the ability to change our future." She squeezed my hand. "Remember that. Nothing is set in stone, not even history. You talking to me now is changing history because when you, Danny and I first time-shifted we never had this advantage. So use it, learn from us and remember anything is possible." She reached into the front pocket of her bag and brought out a large circular locket similar to the one she wore. She put it over my head and tucked it beneath the neckline of my dress. "In case you need our help even when we're not around. I know it doesn't seem like it at the moment but you've been a great friend to me. Thank you." She hugged me. I didn't know what to say and then I heard Danny shouting my name from somewhere in the house. "Keep strong, Maisie," she said. "You're what keeps us together and gives us hope." She released me and stepped away from the bed. "Stand by the door."

"Wait, you're leaving?"

"You'll be fine. But wait until you're somewhere safe before telling the others about this conversation. Don't hang about here. Also, London Bridge is already destroyed. You'll have to cross the river by boat."

"Maisie!" Danny was on the top landing now.

"I'm coming!" I shouted and when I turned back future Lizzie was gone. I reached for the locket and felt its comforting weight beneath my dress. Suddenly I was very aware of the roar of flames close by and the shouts, screams and wails from the street. Holding Charlie tightly I ran out of the room and straight into Danny.

He staggered back. "What's taken you so long?"

"I'll tell you later. I've found Charlie."

"She's freaking out down there worrying about this dog. The fire's only a few houses away."

I clattered after him and the house became darker and stuffier the further down the stairs we went. We burst through the front door and the calmness I'd felt in the top bedroom was shattered by an explosion of noise, glass smashing in the houses already on fire and the deafening roar of flames and splintering wood as it was gobbled up by the fire.

Charlie trembled in my arms. The old man was on the cart with the pregnant lady crying next to him while Lizzie tried to keep her calm.

"Lizzie!" I shouted. "Give her the dog." I passed Charlie up to Lizzie who grabbed him awkwardly.

"Ouch!" she screamed and dropped him on to the wooden bench. "Stupid dog bit me."

"Thank you, thank you so much," the lady said, nuzzling into Charlie's soft fur.

"Lizzie, get down, we're walking."

"It hurts so much," she said, holding her hand out where two specks of blood had appeared.

"You're not going to die from that," I said and thought how right and more sensible Lizzie's older self was. That at least was something to look forward to: Lizzie growing up.

Behind us there was an enormous rumble like the sky was about to fall in on our heads. I turned in time to see a house engulfed in flames disintegrate and crash into the street sending burning timbers flying.

Danny pushed me and Lizzie forwards. "Run!"

Chapter Twenty-Three

I didn't look back. People screaming and the roar of flames filled my ears and the stench of smoke choked my lungs. Women, children, dogs, even the men in uniform who'd been attempting to put out the fire were running for their lives. Danny, Lizzie and me weaved in and out. We ran past people laden with belongings and dodged furniture lying in the street. Charlie, I suddenly thought. I turned back and strained to see the miserable old man and his cart with the lady and Charlie next to him steadily making their way to safety through the packed street.

"Come here!" a gruff voice shouted from the doorway of the nearest house.

A tall thin boy shot into me like a bullet, sending me sprawling to the ground. He stumbled and nearly dropped the necklace he was clutching in his hand but regained his balance and disappeared in the crowd. Dirty cobblestones pounded by strangers' feet, millimetres from my face, stretched in front of me. The palms of my hands were sore and grazed and my knees stung. I tried to scramble to my feet but I was knocked back down by a thick-set man too busy getting out of the fire's way to notice me.

"Danny, wait!" Lizzie shouted, and then I saw her battered fifteenth-century shoes in front of me. She grabbed me beneath my arms and helped me to my feet.

"Are you okay?" she asked as we ducked beneath the overhang of the nearest building.

"Where's Danny?"

"I don't think he saw you fall. Come on," she said, taking my hand. "He'll stop when he realises we're not with him."

We rejoined the flow of people. The fire greedily engulfed each house one by one but it was a good distance behind us now. We reached a crossroads where a group of important-looking men stood in the middle of the road shouting orders. They were dressed in long red coats with breeches tucked into stockings and curly wigs on their heads. At least two of the group had lost their wigs revealing very short hair and their shirts and stockings were no longer white but stained grey with soot.

I pulled Lizzie into the shadow of an imposing building at the corner of the crossroads. "If we go any further we'll lose Danny for good."

"Yeah, well, we can't see a thing with this many people about."

"Give me a piggy back," I said.

She shot me her usual are-you-crazy look and I immediately thought of future Lizzie.

"So I can see over the crowd and find Danny."

She reluctantly turned round and I took a run up and jumped on her back.

"You're too heavy," she said.

"The quicker you turn round and face the road, the sooner I'll be able to get down." I strained my neck to look across the crowded crossroads.

"Hurry up."

The King's men were barricading the road we'd just come down and the one next to it and directing people away from the fire. I caught sight of the old man and the lady with Charlie still on her knee, crawling along in the middle of the crowd, heading towards the road that led to the London gates.

Danny could be anywhere. He could already be on the road heading towards the Thames or he could have tripped like me and be trampled beneath all these feet.

"You're seriously hurting me now," Lizzie said.

"One more minute."

Someone was standing on the steps of the church opposite us, waving madly.

"There he is!" I waved back and Danny pointed to us and then to himself. I nodded and put my thumbs up in reply. I slid off Lizzie's back and put my feet firmly on the cobbles. "He's by the church."

I linked my arm in hers and she didn't pull away. We rejoined the flow of people, skirting the important-looking men dealing with the fire. I could see the cross on St Paul's and the tower behind looming above the houses in front of us.

"What happened?" Danny asked when we reached him.

"Someone knocked into me and I fell."

"I'm so sorry, I didn't see. Are you okay?"

"Only bruises and grazed palms." I held my

hands up.

"No one cared when that dog bit me," Lizzie said.

There was another massive rumble and plumes of smoke puffed into the sky behind us joining the smoky haze clouding the sun.

"So where do we go?" Danny shouted above a second rumble.

I'd visualised the route I thought we should take to the Thames when looking at the map with Lizzie in the attic bedroom. "We need to get to the end of this road," I shouted. "And then turn left towards the river to a road called Thames Street. We'll be able to see how we can cross the river from there."

With Lizzie holding my hand and Danny behind her, I followed the flow of people over the crossroads, past the King's men and on to a very packed Watling Street. I was dying to tell them about my conversation with future Lizzie but there was no time and no safe place to stop. I couldn't wait to see Lizzie's face when she found out I'd spent time with her future self.

Even though we couldn't see the fire any longer we could still hear its roar and the splintering noise as buildings collapsed. Flakes of ash floated down on to the street like grey snowflakes. Shops, inns and houses were being closed up and what must normally have been a thriving London street, full of people bartering and selling, was filled with panic and desperation as shopkeepers' goods were loaded on to carts.

We reached another crossroads and turned left on to Old Change where a row of large houses gave way to the entrance to St Paul's Cathedral on our right. We'd only caught a brief glimpse of it from the cart on the way in but now the sight of it made all three of us stop. Where we stood would soon be scorched earth. The ornate pillars at the front of the cathedral, the brickwork, its towers and spires would very soon be turned to rubble. I walked on, wanting more and more to get across to the other side of the river and leave the destruction behind. There was so much of what future Lizzie had said buzzing around my head, I didn't know what to think any more.

People pushed past us, their arms loaded with books, paintings and chests, heading towards the open doors of the cathedral. At least they still had hope. Talking to future Lizzie had left me feeling positive to begin with but now I was worried and really wanted to get to safety. I didn't like the thought of our success in getting back to Warwick Castle at the exact moment we'd time-shifted being down to me. It was also up to me to get the three of us to the cottage on the other side of the river in one piece. I kept walking, trying not to breathe in the choking stench of human waste running along the drains at the edge of the street. Booksellers and printers were shutting their shops and families were leaving their homes. Everywhere buildings were being emptied and the Londoners' urgency made me walk faster.

The road to the river was packed with people

of all ages, young and old, jostling each other. Women leant out of second-floor windows, shouting across the street to each other about whether they should move their belongings now or wait. We seemed to be the only ones not carrying anything. Roads merged with the one we were on and that meant more people, belongings, horses and carts and we were forced to walk slower and slower.

"No one's moving up ahead," Danny said, standing on tiptoes.

A wider road cut across the one we were on. I studied the map. "That's got to be Thames Street. Come on." I pushed my way through the bottleneck of people, checking every few seconds that Danny and Lizzie were still behind me, until I was forced to stop at the edge of Thames Street where no one could move any further. I backtracked to the side of the road and we stood on the steps of the corner house.

People had formed a chain and were heaving what looked like buckets and bowls of water from the river up towards the houses that were on fire. Thames Street itself was packed with people and I could see no way through.

A tall lanky boy with dark hair squeezed past us on the steps. "Excuse me," I said, grabbing his shoulder. "Excuse me."

He stopped and turned to me. He looked about fifteen or sixteen and he wore expensive-looking clothes but he was sweating and his white shirt, dirtied with soot, showed beneath an unbuttoned green jacket.

He looked me up and down and I felt myself blush, conscious of my now old-fashioned dress. "What can I do for you?" he said.

"Um," I said. "We need to get to the river, is there a way through?"

"It's like this all the way along Thames Street," he said. "Right down to the wharves that haven't burnt yet."

Danny stepped forward so he was next to me. "How can we get to the bridge then?"

The boy laughed. "My friend, the houses on the bridge caught fire yesterday, you won't be crossing the river that way."

"Do you know a way we can get to the river then?" I asked.

He glanced from me to Lizzie. "I'm heading to Fleet Street, if you want to follow me. I can show you the way to Blackfriars Stairs that should avoid all this." He held out his hand and I shook it. "My name's Joseph."

"Maisie," I said. "And this is Danny and Lizzie."

Staying close behind Joseph, we followed him back through the crowd of people we'd just fought our way through.

"You're not from London, are you?" Joseph asked me as the crowds thinned out further up the cobbled road.

"No," I said. "We're from Warwick."

"What brings you here?"

"Family. They live on the other side of the

river. In Southwark."

Lizzie nudged me. "We're from Warwick now, are we?" she said under her breath.

"Why not?" I said. "It's where we're trying to get back to. Warwick Castle on the 21st March 2012 is home after all."

We reached St Paul's and followed Joseph into the cathedral grounds. People hurried between the shops and the cathedral with armloads of books and papers. We veered to the left and followed the path that ran alongside the cathedral wall.

Ludgate Hill was jam-packed with timber-framed houses and shops that went uphill towards another city gate. The street here was still filled with people but no one rushed about or dragged furniture from houses like they'd done on the roads where the fire was chasing people out of their homes. We passed a road on our right and my heart thudded against my ribs. The plaque on the wall of the corner house said "Warwick Lane". We had to get back. We couldn't spend the rest of our lives wandering aimlessly through time.

Just before Ludgate, Joseph stopped and pointed to the road on our left. "Keep heading downhill and you'll reach the river," he said. He gave a slight bow. "Pleasure meeting you."

"Thank you, Joseph!" I called after him.

"*Thank you, Joseph!*" Lizzie fluttered her eyelashes at me.

"What?" I said.

"You so fancy him."

"No I don't."

"He was posh and full of himself," Danny said, walking past us.

"Ooh, someone's jealous," Lizzie said.

~

The Thames was the colour of mud and stank of wet dog. From Blackfriars Stairs we could see all the way along the north side of the river and just how far the fire had already spread. Even this far down, boats were crammed against the bank as Londoners passed household items down to people in the boats or simply threw them into the water. The murky river was wide, much wider than I thought it would be. Houses and buildings lined the opposite bank but were less clustered together than on this side of the river. And then further downstream I saw London Bridge, tightly packed with tall houses built on the bridge itself. They must have once looked impressive but now they were a crumbling mass of blackened wood and collapsed roofs. The bridge was no longer on fire but the burnt buildings still smoked.

"There really is only one way to cross then," Danny said.

"No way am I swimming," Lizzie said, folding her arms across her chest.

"We're not going to swim." Danny pointed to the boats clustered together further down the bank.

Among all the other boats and barges being loaded with goods and people, there was a small empty boat. Nobody seemed to be claiming it. I saw our chance, "Come on!"

We weaved in and out of people and ducked beneath chests and tables that were being lowered to the boats. We reached the quieter end of Blackfriars where the bank gave way to the river and realised we had to step across two other boats already filled with people and belongings to reach the empty one.

"You have to be joking," Lizzie said. "We're going to end up falling in and getting crushed between the other boats."

"Then don't fall in," Danny said, leaving the safety of the bank for the wooden edge of the first boat and politely saying "excuse me" before hopping across to the next boat.

"Step where I step and you'll be fine," I said.

Lizzie followed so closely behind me I could feel her breath on my neck as we stepped on to the first boat. I ignored the grumbles of the men in the second boat as we stepped across and left it rocking. We made it to the empty boat and my feet landed in water.

"Now we know why it's empty," I said, looking at the large puddle in the bottom of the boat.

Danny held up an oar. "And only one of these." He sat down on one of the two benches either side of the puddle. "Let's go before we sink."

"Too late, there's already more water coming in," Lizzie said. She lifted the bottom of her dress out of the water to reveal her soaking feet.

There were too many other boats by the banks of the Thames to move anywhere quickly. I navigated, Danny paddled with the one oar and

Lizzie bailed the water from the bottom of our boat using a wooden bowl she'd found floating in the river. Even though we weren't that far out into the Thames we could see all of the damage caused by the fire. Everything to the east of us along the river was burnt or on fire. Flames jumped into the air and a thick blanket of smoke hovered above London completely blotting out the sun and sky. It looked like a scene from a disaster movie.

"We need another bowl," Lizzie said. She tipped brown water over the side. "It's coming in faster than I can get it out."

I rolled up my sleeves and with my hands cupped together started scooping out the river water in the bottom of the boat. Danny paddled as fast as he could but bigger boats kept knocking into us. It was a long way to the opposite riverbank and it seemed impossible to reach in a leaking boat. We fought our way through the mass of boats gathered at the river's edge until we had more space to manoeuvre, although we were a bit lopsided with only one oar.

Lizzie tipped another bowlful of brown water over the side and looked towards London. "We were in the middle of that a while ago. I still keep thinking we're going to wake up at home any second."

"I wish," I said.

"Maisie, I need you to help me paddle straight. Grab a piece of wood to use as an oar. Lizzie, bail out faster."

"I'm going as fast as I can. It's making me feel sick."

Danny glanced at me and raised an eyebrow.

"You'll believe me when I puke all over you." She slammed the bowl into the water on the floor of the boat and chucked it back into the river.

I sat back on the seat next to Danny and searched the water for something oar-like. It seemed as if the whole of London was floating in the river: soggy books, barrels, wooden plates and bowls and charred bits of wood that probably only a few hours ago were part of a house. I spied a piece of flat wide wood floating by. I leant over the side of the boat and plucked it from the river. I dipped my makeshift oar into the water and started to help Danny row us across to the south bank in a straight line.

Lizzie stopped bailing out water and wiped her forehead with the sleeve of her dress. She looked pale. She shuffled about on her seat.

"Are you okay?" I asked.

She shook her head slowly. "I feel horrible."

Even in the brief time she'd stopped bailing, the bottom of the boat rapidly filled with water.

She stood up and chucked the bowl at my feet. "Swap with me."

"Okay," I said. "But go slowly."

She started to clamber across the boat.

"Stop moving, Lizzie!" Danny shouted.

"I can't sit backwards any longer. I'm going to be sick."

"Stop rocking!"

"Seriously, I'm gonna be sick." She stumbled on the edge of the wooden seat next to Danny, put her hand out to steady herself but missed the edge of the boat. I reached out but only managed to snatch the hem of her dress before she tumbled head first with a huge splash into the Thames. And then she wasn't there anymore, only sludgy water sloshed around where she'd fallen.

"Danny!" I shouted as the oar slipped from his hand. He grabbed hold of it before it too disappeared into the water. We both stared at the spot in the river where Lizzie had been and then looked at each other.

"She time-shifted, right?" Danny said. "She didn't just sink?"

I looked at the bowl she'd just passed to me for bailing out the water and nodded. "She time-shifted all right."

Chapter Twenty-Four

Future Lizzie had warned me we could change history and our future, but this was all wrong – this wasn't supposed to happen. We'd lost Lizzie here, now in 1666. Floating in the middle of the Thames in a sinking boat with London burning behind us, things couldn't get any worse.

"I'm going in after her," I said.

"Don't be stupid." Danny pushed me back on to the seat. "You'll sink in that dress."

"We can't just do nothing."

Danny placed the oar on the seat next to me. "If I time-shift, follow me."

"No Danny, wait!"

He dived into the Thames. There was a huge splash and I held my breath, willing him to reappear but ready to jump in after him if he didn't. He surfaced, spat out a mouthful of water and paddled back to the boat. "That didn't work."

He leant on the side of the boat and between us he managed to drag himself back in, although it was just as wet inside the boat as it was out.

"We're both going to be swimming in a minute," I said and started to bail out water again.

I couldn't believe Lizzie was gone. All the times over the past few days I'd wished she wasn't with me, I took it all back now.

Dripping water on the seat, Danny ran his

hands through his soaking hair. He always had his hair spiky at the front and my brother Ollie would tease him about using as much hair product as a girl. I chucked another bowlful of water over the side.

"What do we do now?" he asked.

"I don't know." I bailed faster. Our plan and what future Lizzie had said had all fallen apart. I looked at the brown water I chucked over the side. "I hope you didn't swallow any of this."

Danny sat back down on the bench. "Maisie, we've got to do something. I don't like Lizzie but there's no way we can go home without her."

I looked past him to the boats being loaded on the banks of the Thames and the fire engulfing the buildings and church spires of London. "We won't go home without her. We can't. But if we can't join Lizzie then we should at least get ourselves to safety first and then figure out what to do."

Danny nodded and picked up the oar and the bit of driftwood I'd taken from the river and started to row towards the south bank. We were only a little more than halfway across and I was certain we'd sink before reaching the other side. I kept bailing out the water. Where had Lizzie time-shifted? She'd be terrified on her own. I choked back tears. How could future Lizzie be so sure I'd get us all back home when I'd already failed her? I dripped tears into the murky water but Danny was too busy battling against the river to notice.

~

Our leaking boat made it to the south bank of the Thames and we jumped out on to the grassy bank and let the boat float away. To the west the sun was beginning to dip and although the sky behind us was a clear blue, the black clouds above London gave the impression of darkness. London really was burning now and the whole skyline was lit red and orange.

"There's something I need to tell you before we do anything." I sat down on the riverbank and waited for Danny to join me. I told him about my surprise meeting with future Lizzie in the attic room. I told him how long our future selves had been time-shifting for, and how future Lizzie had explained how we had the ability to change our history and future. Lastly I showed him Robbie's map where future Lizzie had marked an X where the cottage was.

Danny shifted himself into a cross-legged position on the grass and studied the map. "So Lizzie time-shifting in the middle of the Thames didn't happen when our future selves originally time-shifted, did it?"

"No, but..."

"So does that mean we've already changed our future?"

I scrunched up my face. "I have no idea. But I guess everything we do will affect our future and losing Lizzie now when we're so close to the possibility of getting home is like a massive problem."

"Then Lizzie time-shifting in the middle of the

Thames wasn't supposed to happen otherwise future Lizzie would have warned you." He paused and frowned. "So if they've been wandering about in time for the last fourteen years and think this spot here," he pointed at the new X on the map, "is our best chance of getting back to the same day in 2012 we were first time-shifted from, then Lizzie disappearing has really messed things up, hasn't it?"

"Basically, yes."

"We always talked about wanting an adventure," he said quietly.

"Yeah, but not one quite as real as this."

I plucked at the grass and watched the river glowing red and orange from the flames as it flowed past. "I think we've only got two options," I said slowly. "The first is to get back on the Thames and somehow hope we can time-shift to the same time Lizzie's been shifted, whenever that is. Or secondly we head to this cottage, pick up the rucksack they left for us, get back to our own time and figure out how we can help Lizzie then."

"It's pointless us all being lost in time. What would Lizzie do?"

I looked at him and smiled. "She'd take the second option. Go home, of course."

"That's decided. We'll go home and find a way to help her then. Maybe they'll find us again. You know, our future selves."

I stood up and shook off the grass stuck to my damp dress. We walked up the bank to the first row of houses in Southwark and I felt as if we'd abandoned her out there in the Thames, but the truth was she wasn't even here in 1666. We couldn't chase after her like me and Lizzie had done after Danny and the army. I couldn't time-shift to any time or place at will like my future self supposedly could.

~

Southwark was almost as built-up as London. Timber-framed houses backed on to the river and we walked along a narrow road that we hoped would lead to London Bridge.

The sun was beginning to set and it was the first time all day that it hadn't been hidden by smoke and flames. Because the sky was darkening, the fire seemed to be even bigger and brighter. Between the houses we caught glimpses of flames leaping high above London, reflected red and gold in the Thames.

The dirt and stones of the road caught in the hem of my dress but it was too heavy to lift off the ground all the time. I would have done anything for trainers, shorts and a T-shirt instead of this stupid dress.

The further into Southwark we walked, the more houses there were and the stronger the stench of human waste and stuff rotting in the narrow channels running on each side of the road.

Danny spluttered and coughed. "This smell is so much worse than your farm."

"Our farm doesn't smell," I said, covering my nose with my hands in an attempt to filter out the stench.

"You're used to it, that's why. Maybe we'll get used to smelling human poo too."

"I hope not."

We'd walked a good way and we were both hot and sweaty when the houses gave way to a large, dirt-ingrained building right on the Thames with a sign "The Clink" above the iron gates. A shoeless skinny kid scrabbled around in the dirt and women with big skirts and low-cut corsets called out to men as they passed. We hurried on, glimpsing the bridge and the destroyed part of London on the opposite bank as we crossed a wide road.

"I wonder where Lizzie is," Danny said, as we pressed ourselves against a wall of a house as a large wagon filled with barrels trundled by.

"You've never worried about Lizzie before."

"I'm not *worried* about her," he said. "It's just I know what it's like to be time-shifted on your own."

I bit my lip. "I'm sorry, I didn't mean to be nasty."

"You're not being nasty, don't worry. You've got a long way to go to be as mean as Lizzie is."

"I am worried about her though," I said.

He nodded. "It's scary out there on your own."

I squeezed his arm. "If it was scary for you, I've no idea how Lizzie will cope without us."

The main London road appeared in front of us filled with people and horses unable to cross the bridge into the city. The King's men guarded the bridge and the burnt houses on the bridge itself still smoked. The bitter smell of charred wood stung my nostrils. I swallowed back bile but not because of the smell. On either side of the bridge stuck on spikes were two human heads. There were dark sockets where their eyes had been. Crows hovered above darting down to pick at what rotting flesh remained.

I grabbed hold of Danny who was looking the other way. "That's just sick," I said and pointed.

He looked towards the bridge and smiled. "Cool. That's what I wanted to see in Warwick Castle's dungeon."

I shook my head. "Unbelievable. Did you not see enough at the Battle of Barnet?"

His smile faded. "That was different."

"How?"

"I don't want to talk about it."

"Okay, I'm sorry."

"Let me see the map."

I pulled it out of my pouch and handed it to him. I hadn't thought to ask him how he was feeling or what he'd done or seen during the battle but I should have.

"I don't reckon it's too far to the cottage." He handed me the map and set off along the road, heading away from the fire, the burnt bridge and the heads on spikes.

I jogged a few steps to catch up with him. "If you want to talk about what happened you can, you know."

"It wasn't so much what I saw during the battle or what I had to do," Danny said. "Although that was pretty sick and I saw some of the soldiers I'd marched with die on the battlefield... It was more the fact I was on my own and I had no idea what had happened. I couldn't remember the first couple of hours anyway and then I was just confused about what was going on. You will never realise how happy I was to see you. I was even pleased to see Lizzie until she opened her mouth."

We passed loads of inns and houses and finally the timber-framed buildings gave way to trees, fields and occasional cottages. The sky ahead was darkening but flames lit up the grey, smoke-filled sky behind us.

"What are we looking for?" Danny asked.

"A tree in the middle of the road and then the cottage is down a dirt track on the left."

"And the bag's inside the cottage?"

"That's what she said. It's one of the houses they use when time-shifting. She called it a safe house."

"Doesn't it seem odd that they've gone to all this trouble for us to collect this bag when she could have given it to you in London?"

I kicked at the dirt on the road. My head pounded. "Everything's odd, Danny. The whole situation. I mean, why did future Lizzie talk to just me? As for why she didn't give the bag to me then, maybe she thought it wasn't safe as we were in the middle of the fire at the time. Anyway, the cottage is the place we need to get to if we want to time-shift home, so really it's the best place for us to collect the bag."

"I don't like the fact it was just Lizzie who talked to you and not us. How do you know we were safe?"

"I know you don't like Lizzie but that's no reason not to trust her. She's different as an adult. She's not a bad person."

Danny huffed and we walked on in silence. As the darkness grew I concentrated harder on the road ahead. It was so still and quiet. We hadn't seen anyone for ages because no one was able to get in or out of London via the bridge.

The oak tree was impossible to miss, looming dark against the moonlit sky with the road curving round it. A track on our left led off the road into a wood and I was beginning to wonder if we'd gone the wrong way when the whitewashed walls of a cottage appeared, just as future Lizzie had promised. Its windows were dark and there didn't seem to be anyone about. It was hidden from the road by the wood, but I still shivered as we crept up to the wooden door.

"Look." Danny traced his fingers over the letters M, D, L carved into the wood. "Maisie, Danny and Lizzie," he whispered. He turned the handle. "Locked." He shook his head. "They went to all this trouble but didn't give us a key to get in." He ran his hand along the top of the doorframe.

"Wait," I said, pulling the necklace Lizzie had given me from beneath my dress. I clicked the clasp of the locket open and a key dropped into my palm.

"Okay, maybe they have thought of everything," Danny said as I slotted the key into the lock, turned it until it clicked and pushed the door open.

Chapter Twenty-Five

It was even darker inside than out. "Keep the door open so I can see," I said to Danny as he followed me in. I could just make out a large table in the middle of the room. I headed for it. There was a lantern on it and as I ran my hands along the table in front of it my fingers found a plastic lighter. I ignited the gas and lit the candle inside the lantern. A flickering light bathed the room in warmth.

Danny closed the door. "So this is their safe house," he said as he studied the books on the shelves near the front door. "Look at these, every history book you could ever want." He took a book about the Great Fire of London off the shelf and thumbed through it.

The table was bare apart from the lantern and lighter. Opposite the front door was a large fireplace with a cooking pot hanging above it. On either side of the fireplace were wooden shelves.

"Danny, look."

He left the book on the table and joined me. The shelves were filled with tins of soup and stew, packets of long-life mashed potato, baked beans and tuna.

"We're going to have a feast," Danny said.

In a cupboard by the front door I found a camping stove, gas bottles, a couple of saucepans, cutlery, plates and bowls, and the last cupboard held a first-aid kit, lots of plasters, safety pins, paracetamol and hay fever tablets. It took me right back to the locked room in Robbie's house with his stash of twenty-first-century necessities and luxuries.

"It gets better, Maisie," Danny said from the other side of the room. He stood in the doorway of a bedroom with three single beds, all made up with duvets and pillows that looked so inviting. Danny launched himself on to the first bed and laughed. "This is amazing!"

The rucksack was on the middle bed. I unzipped the main pocket and reached in and pulled out a stack of freshly made sandwiches and a bag of doughnuts.

The front pocket contained what Lizzie had promised: three Tube tickets dated 21/03/12 and three train tickets from London Victoria to Warwick. I held the tickets in my hands and smiled. I was holding on to a piece of home. I turned around to show Danny but he was already asleep. Along with a change of clothes for each of us, there was a Tube map, an A-Z of London, a train timetable and a mobile phone but a couple of other things like a lighter, toothbrushes, toothpaste, deodorant and a first-aid kit puzzled me.

I took a doughnut from the bag and left Danny sleeping. I sat at the table next to the unlit fire and took a bite of the doughnut. Nothing had ever tasted so good. I tried not to lick my lips but after the third mouthful I had to. The sugar kick was insane and when I bit into the jam it was the best thing I'd tasted in days – apart from Robbie's pheasant casserole and Hannah's roast dinner. I licked my fingers and looked around the room. I didn't get how we were supposed to just time-shift from here but future Lizzie had been so sure. I was puzzled about so many things. Was this cottage where our future selves lived when we weren't shifting through time? I suppose it was the kind of place that remained standing for three or four hundred years. I rested my head on my arms and thought of home.

~

It could have been branches creaking in the wind or Danny stirring but I woke suddenly, my neck stiff where I'd been resting on the table. Daylight streamed through the small window. I went to blow out the candle but it had already melted to nothing. I tiptoed to the bedroom and opened the door. Danny was lying in bed with his hands tucked beneath his head and his eyes open.

"We're still here then," he said.

"It seems that way."

"Haven't you slept?"

"I did; I fell asleep at the table."

"You missed out sleeping in your own bed. This is my bed, literally," he said, pointing at the "D" carved into the wood of the headboard.

I looked at the headboard of the middle bed with the rucksack and smiled when I saw the letter "M". "I'd have chosen this bed."

"Well obviously, because you did choose it." He sat up and stretched. "I'm starving."

"Me too. There's a tin of sausages and baked beans on the shelf."

Danny groaned and swung his legs off the bed.

"There are clean clothes in the rucksack," I said.

"Like clean old-fashioned clothes?"

"Like clean comfy modern clothes."

I couldn't wait to get out of my hot scratchy dress but I wanted to wash first. I slipped outside. It was very early in the morning but it already felt warm. I splashed my face with cold fresh water from the well and washed my hair not caring how curly it would go once it dried. Birds sung in the trees that surrounded the cottage. Above the treetops smoke still hovered over London. There was no doubt that we were still in 1666.

Danny was emptying a tin of beans and sausages into a saucepan when I went back in. He turned round. "What do you think?"

He'd put on the clothes from the rucksack: dark grey combat trousers, trainers and a black hooded top.

"You look normal."

He grinned at me. "It seriously feels amazing. Go get changed and then we can eat breakfast."

Danny had put the clothes meant for me and Lizzie out on my bed. I chose black combats, a green vest-top and grey canvas trainers. It was like a huge weight had dropped off me changing from the dress into familiar clothes. We were now ready to time-shift home and I hoped it would happen quickly because I didn't fancy putting the dress back on any time soon. I stuffed Lizzie's clothes and my hooded top back into the rucksack, zipped it up and took it with me into the main room.

I sat down at the table and Danny placed a bowl of steaming baked beans and sausages in front of me. We ate greedily, burning our tongues because we couldn't wait to let the beans cool down.

"I could get used to this," Danny said.

"What, baked beans for breakfast?"

"This life. You know the freedom of time-shifting."

"You're kidding, right?"

He shook his head. "What have we got to look forward to back home? School? Exams? Homework? Lizzie and her friends making our lives miserable? Do you really want to grow up, get a boring job and work for the rest of your life until you're too old to enjoy anything anymore?"

"There are our families, our camping trip in the summer..."

"That seems a bit pathetic after all this, it's not exactly an adventure, is it?"

I scraped my chair back and stood up. "You'd rather be wandering about through time having an adventure than ever getting home again?"

"Wouldn't you?"

"No. What about our families? What do you think they're going through right now?" I slammed my empty bowl on the shelf above the fireplace. "You're so selfish."

There was a loud familiar rumble and I stumbled forwards as the flagstones beneath my feet shook. Danny reached out and grabbed my hand.

"Did you really mean what you said?" I shouted over the rumble.

He shook his head and his grin returned. "Of course I want to get home, it just doesn't mean I'm not enjoying myself."

A crack appeared in the wall next to the door.

"The rucksack!" Danny shouted.

It was on the table, which shuddered with the force of the earth shifting. Gripping on to Danny I launched myself forwards, stretching my hand out until I clasped a canvas strap. Then there was air beneath me and I couldn't see anything, but sensed we were falling... We thudded on to the ground and I carefully stretched my hand out on to something damp and spiky. Grass. It was cold, much colder. I opened my eyes and saw Danny, the rucksack and a lawn in the back garden of a terraced house.

Chapter Twenty-Six

We'd time-shifted, just as future Lizzie said we would. Behind us was a garden shed and next to us a red painted swing. A neat lawn led up to a decked area and the back of a terraced house.

"We did it," Danny said.

"Thanks to you winding me up."

"That's easy enough to do."

I whacked his arm. "Don't start, we don't want to be time-shifted again."

We stood up and shook damp grass off ourselves.

"It's freezing." I reached into the rucksack and pulled out the green hooded top and put it on. I peered at the house whose garden we'd ended up in. "We're in a row of terraced houses, how are we supposed to get out?"

"Look, two doors up, they've got a side entrance," Danny said, swinging the rucksack on his back.

It had to be morning, and I hoped the people who lived here were at work or school. We clambered over the first fence and landed in a border filled with plants that we tried not to trample on before we nipped across the lawn and over a low wall into the garden with the side entrance. This garden was overgrown and weeds poked through the patio slabs where a rusty barbecue was filled with water.

A window scraped open on the first floor. "Oi!" a young man shouted. "What're you doing?"

"Go, go!" Danny said and we legged it across the patio and down the side of the house. A locked gate was between us and the road, but we were able to heave ourselves up on to the garden wall and squeeze past it and out on to the pavement. We turned left and ran along the pavement, not looking back when we heard another shout from the house. I caught sight of cars, lampposts, telephone poles and street signs as we ran – all things I'd never usually pay attention to but I was so happy to see now.

We stopped when we reached the crossroads at the end of the road.

"He hasn't followed us," Danny said between breaths. "Maybe he realised there wasn't anything worth nicking in that garden anyway."

I caught my breath and reached into the front pocket of the rucksack and pulled out the London A-Z. "We need to find Borough Tube station." I'd never been to London before – the biggest city I'd ever been to was Cardiff and that was with Mum, Dad and Ollie when we visited my grandparents, so really that didn't count.

"I'll find it," Danny said, taking the A-Z from me. "What's the name of this main road... Borough High Street." He flicked through the pages. "So it can't be far..."

Cars crawled to a stop at the traffic lights and both sides of the road were choked up. People barged past each other, most of them talking on their mobiles. The smell of bacon and egg wafted into the street from the café on the corner. It was the first time in the last few days I'd felt out of my depth. Did I actually miss what we'd just left behind? A car parallel to us slammed its brakes on and honked its horn. I realised what I missed: our farm, the quietness of the countryside away from car fumes and noise. That's what I'd liked about the past.

Danny tapped his finger on a page in the A-Z. "It's a bit further up on the other side of this road."

I was glad Danny was leading this time. I'd been the one leading the way in 1471 and again in 1666 but now everything was a blur. Familiar things like hairdressers, McDonald's, newsagents and a butcher's shop were all in an unfamiliar place. We shouldn't be walking around London on our own, it was a weekday and we should be in school. Were people looking at us strangely? Maybe someone would report us. We were truants, knocking off school for the day, except we'd actually been gone for over a week.

"Look, there's the Tube station." Danny pointed ahead.

"Do you think we've made the wrong decision?" I asked. My feet felt like lead pounding the last bit of pavement. "How are we going to explain why Lizzie's not with us?"

Danny shrugged. "We make it up as we go along, I guess."

The clock in the Tube station said 10.17. "Do

you realise that at the moment me, you and Lizzie are on the coach heading to Warwick."

Danny shook his head. "Seriously, Maisie, you're going to make my head explode. Get the tickets out." He turned his back to me so I could reach into the rucksack pocket. I took them and the Tube map out.

I looked at the maze of coloured lines. "How are we ever going to find our way to Victoria?" There were a couple of people queuing at the ticket office and a few more people waiting at the automated machines in the middle of the Tube entrance.

Danny snatched the Tube map off me and studied it. "We're here," he pointed to where it said Borough, "and we have to get here." He ran his finger along the Tube line to Victoria.

"Your tongue's hanging out," I said.

"I'm concentrating," he said and stuck his tongue out properly at me. "We have to change on to either the Circle or District line. Come on, it's only two stops away." He took one of the tickets from me.

We headed for the gates and Danny slipped his ticket into the slot. Beep, beep, beep. Error it stated on the screen.

"Try yours."

Beep, beep, beep.

"Problem?" the guard by the end machine asked.

"Our tickets won't let us through," I said.

"Where are you going?" He flicked his fingers

and I handed him the tickets.

"Victoria."

He glanced at our tickets and was about to open the gate for us when he frowned and looked at them again. "They're four years out of date."

"What?" Danny and me said together.

The guard pointed at the date and then smiled. "Ha, good one, good April Fool."

"It's not 21st March 2012 then?"

"Er, no. It's 1st April 2016." He handed the tickets back to me and chuckled. "Nice one," he said as he walked off.

"How can it possibly be 2016?" Danny asked.

"I have no idea."

"We have money right? To buy tickets?"

"What good will that do if we're four years in the future? Wait a second." I jogged over to the newsagent by the entrance. I picked up the top copy from a pile of *Sun* newspapers on a stand and read the date: Friday 1st April 2016.

Danny peered over my shoulder. "I don't get it. How did we end up here?"

"Maisie. Danny," said a familiar voice behind us.

I knew it was future Lizzie even before I turned around.

She was dressed all in black again with a headscarf tying her blonde hair back off her face. She took the newspaper from my hand and put it back. "I told you a little white lie, I'm sorry."

"A little lie?" I said. "We're four years in the future."

Danny folded his arms across his chest and stepped forward. "Maisie told me you'd turned into a better person as a grown-up. But you tricked us so I guess she was misled. Why would you do this to us?"

"I'm probably not the best person to be explaining the reasons why to you." She stepped back. Leaning against the opposite wall at the entrance of the Tube station were a man and woman. I gasped and Danny gripped my arm tightly. I still had mad curly hair but it was held off my face with a black band and the curls were neater. I was tall but had grown into my lankiness and didn't look awkward anymore. I barely recognised Danny who was much taller with muscles and a lot of stubble. They walked over to us and we stared face to face with ourselves. Danny didn't have his baby face any longer but his smiling hazel eyes were the same.

"Hey Maisie, hey Danny," my future self said and smiled. "You managed to lose Lizzie then. We've been trying to do that for years."

Future Lizzie whacked her on the arm. "Thanks, mate."

I grabbed Danny's arm and began to walk away. "This is just way too weird."

"Maisie, I'm sorry," my future self said. "We didn't mean to freak you out. Lizzie time-shifting from the Thames on her own messed up everything; we had planned to get all three of you home safely."

"Wait, how do you know about Lizzie time-shifting?" I said.

"I was keeping an eye on you all during the fire and I saw Lizzie time-shift in the middle of the Thames."

"You were following us?"

"Sort of." She glanced around at the people coming in and out of the station. "Please, Maisie, let's go somewhere we can talk properly."

"Fine," I said. "But we want some answers."

We followed future Maisie, Danny and Lizzie out of the Tube station and back on to the street choked with traffic and went into a Starbucks. We sat down with Maisie at a table at the back of the café while future Danny and Lizzie queued up for drinks. Danny watched himself chatting to Lizzie in the queue and frowned.

"It's complicated," Maisie said before either Danny or me had a chance to ask anything.

"I know it's complicated," I said. "I just don't get it. I mean why did Lizzie tell us to get to the cottage when she knew it would take us into the future?"

"Because time-shifting from the actual spot in 1666 to get you to the 21st March 2012 would be as good as suicide."

"I don't get it," Danny said.

Maisie unfolded a map of central London and ran her finger over Southwark. "In 1666 the correct spot to time-shift home is beneath a big old oak tree in the middle of a meadow. But in 2012 that exact same spot is in the middle of Blackfriars Road. The risk is too great. You could time-shift into the path of a lorry."

"We'd have been better off following Robbie's advice," I said.

"No you wouldn't have," Maisie said firmly. She tucked a wayward curl behind her ear and I couldn't help feel ashamed of my mass of curls sticking out in all directions on my head. "Robbie's X on the map is where it all went wrong for us. Lizzie told you the truth about that. We time-shifted to what we thought was the day we'd left but by the time we'd realised that it couldn't be the 21st March because leaves were on the trees and the blossom was out we were already in Warwick. Of course no one from school was there, and when we questioned the gardener at the castle we discovered that we'd been missing for four weeks, presumed dead. Two schoolgirls and a boy fitting the descriptions of the three missing children made the gardener suspicious, so we legged it."

Future Danny reached over us and placed three steaming mugs of coffee on the table. "That's when we time-shifted back to 1471..."

"But after the Battle of Barnet this time," future Lizzie said, sitting down and placing two mugs of hot chocolate with marshmallows in front of me and Maisie.

"So you ended up back where we started?" Danny said. He took a sip of his coffee. "Lush."

Future Danny grinned. "Caramel latte. Our favourite."

I caught a brief knowing look pass between

Maisie and future Lizzie. There was so much history between our older selves, fourteen years of friendship cemented while they wandered through time.

"We made a pact," Maisie said. "We all get home, or none of us does. With your determination and our knowledge, I know it will happen. The idea was, the three of you would time-shift here to 2016 and we'd escort you to Blackfriars Road in the early hours of the morning when it's quieter to make sure you time-shifted home. But obviously that changed. You've got to go after Lizzie first."

"And how do we do that?" I asked.

"We've got you tickets for the ferry to cross the Thames," future Danny said, reaching into his trouser pocket. "It leaves at 1.15pm from Bankside."

"You want us to jump into the Thames?" Danny said spitting out a mouthful of coffee.

Future Danny placed the tickets on the table in front of us. "You'll time-shift, I promise."

"We'll still end up in the river the other end though," Danny said, folding his arms across his chest.

"We wouldn't ask you to do it if it wasn't something we knew you could do," future Danny said.

"What he actually means," future Lizzie said, "is he wouldn't be asking me when I was your age because I'd have totally freaked out." I grinned and future Lizzie laughed. "You two are the adventurous ones. Go have an adventure."

"But be careful," Maisie said. "Well, as careful as you can be. Lizzie's time-shifted to 1730. We have another safe house there on Trinity Lane, number twenty-four. Here's a map of London for this period." She placed a laminated map on the table. "The key inside your locket will open the door."

"How can you be so sure we'll time-shift?" I asked.

Maisie turned the map round so it faced me. "There are certain places where there's a very high chance you'll time-shift without having to do anything. The cottage is one place and, as we're beginning to discover, so is the Thames."

"How come Lizzie didn't fall in and time-shift when you three crossed the Thames?" I asked.

Maisie shrugged. "I didn't spend time talking to Lizzie in the attic bedroom the first time round – we got on a different boat... We're changing history all the time and that makes things unpredictable."

"You've thought of everything."

"We've had fourteen years to figure things out," Maisie said. "What we hadn't planned on was Lizzie getting separated from you. But we know she's okay because we've just left her."

I put my mug of hot chocolate down on the table. "I don't get it – if you've just been with her in 1730, why couldn't you have time-shifted her back here with you, like you time-shifted those riders away?"

Maisie sighed and crossed her arms on the table. "I can time-shift to whenever and wherever I want, but there's no guarantee even with me holding on to Lizzie that she'd end up in the same place as me. I didn't care about those people in the wood getting lost in time or ending up somewhere dangerous but I can't take that risk with Lizzie or any of you. So, the only option is for you to go after her. We took her to our house in Trinity Lane, so she's at least warm and safe until you get there."

"You're not going with us?" Danny asked.

"We're going to help and guide you as much as we can," future Lizzie said. "You're not on your own, but..."

"But there are some things we need to attend to in order to keep you safe," future Danny said.

Danny opened his mouth to say something but closed it again. The five of us fell silent, the only noise being the slurp of coffee and the drone of chatter from elsewhere in the café. "You should tell us what's really going on," I said. "We may be only twelve but you'd have wanted to know the truth when you were our age."

"You're right," Maisie said. "I know you want to know and I know you can handle the truth." She glanced at future Danny and Lizzie and they both nodded. She turned back to us. "Time-shifting gives people the ability to alter the past and change the future and it's big business in the twenty-second century. It's supposed to be regulated by an independent organisation called the International Time Travel Authority or ITTA for short but there are a lot of individuals and companies and black market dealers who have become very rich and powerful exploiting time shifters. You three, us, we're all time shifters and that puts us in danger. We need you to find Lizzie and get home as soon as possible."

"Time travel." I shook my head. "*Time travel* is big business... Unbelievable."

"The future's not important at the moment. The present and getting you all home is what matters."

"We'll find her," Danny said. "Won't we, Maisie?"

"Of course we will." It seemed like an impossible task but we'd walked and ridden for miles in 1471 to find Danny so there was no reason we couldn't do the same again and find Lizzie in eighteenth-century London. At least we were getting closer to home. I took a sip of my marshmallow hot chocolate. 2016. I'd be sixteen years old and doing my GCSEs, how grown-up was that. But in reality, here now in 2016 as far as our parents were concerned we were still missing. Four years on, would they have given up all hope of ever finding us? I shuddered. The longer we spent in the past the further away home felt.

"You've gone very quiet, Maisie," future Lizzie said.

It took a moment to realise she was talking to me. "I'm just thinking."

"About home?"

I nodded and swallowed back tears.

"Good," future Lizzie said, "it's what will keep you going."

"How have you not given up?" Danny asked.

There was a pause as future Maisie, Danny and Lizzie looked at each other. "Because it may not be the life we were supposed to lead, but it is our life," future Danny said. "We've travelled through time and seen the future and that's something very few people have done. And most importantly, after all this time we've figured out how to get ourselves... get you home."

"Fair enough," Danny said. "I always wanted to have an adventure, beats having to go to school."

"You'd better get going," Maisie said, glancing at her watch.

Danny downed the last of his latte. "Thanks for the coffee."

"No problem," future Danny said, and smiled. "You had to start our addiction to caramel lattes sometime."

"It's the one thing he pines for when he's in the past," future Lizzie said, touching his arm.

Maisie scraped her chair back and stood up. She handed me an A4 map with the route to the ferry drawn on it and two bundled up cloaks, which we attached to our belts. I didn't know whether we should hug or something. Maisie reached across the table and squeezed my shoulder. "Be strong, be positive and stick together."

"What do we do when we've found Lizzie?" Danny asked.

"Stick to the original plan," Maisie said. "Get yourselves back to the cottage, time-shift back here to 2016 and we'll meet you."

We left them at the table in Starbucks and returned into smoggy, noisy daylight.

"That was the weirdest half-hour of my life," Danny said.

"Weirder than being time-shifted to 1471 or 1666 or 2016?"

"You don't think talking to ourselves fourteen years older than we are now is the most bizarre thing you've ever done?"

"Everything that's happened this last week has blown my mind. Nothing can surprise me any more."

~

The map was easy to follow, pretty much a straight line to the river on a noisy main road, past cafés, restaurants and shops. Businessmen and women rushed about on their lunch break, in and out of sandwich shops and cafés, except really none of this had even happened yet.

"What did you think of yourself?" Danny asked.

I smiled. "Okay, you're right, it is completely weird. But I liked my hair."

"I looked like I'd been working out."

"You and Lizzie seemed close."

Danny scowled and quickened the pace. "After fourteen years we must have learnt to put up with each other."

~

The Thames glistened in the sunshine. It didn't look as wide as it had in 1666 and its banks were more defined and built up. We sat next to one of the windows on the ferry that looked downstream towards Southwark Bridge. We were close to the doors to the outside deck and although we'd only just left Bankside Pier and we had to get halfway across the river, my heart thudded in my chest.

"How are we going to know if someone's from the future?" Danny asked. "I mean, there could be someone on the ferry now who's after us."

"The man and woman in the wood weren't very subtle." I fidgeted with the edge of the seat and kept watching the bridge to see how far we'd got. "I think we'd know."

"Tickets please," a guard asked passengers a few seats away from us.

I hunted about in my pockets for the tickets.

"We should get outside now," Danny said.

"Tickets please," the ferry guard said as he stopped in front of us. "Shouldn't you kids be in school?"

"In-service training day," Danny said.

"Which school?" he asked.

"We're not from around here," I said quickly.

"Do your parents know where you are?"

"Of course they do."

"How about ringing them now so I can check with them," he said, offering us his mobile.

"Danny..." I nudged his arm. We were nearing the middle of the Thames and I reckoned we had about thirty seconds left before we were in the right place to jump. Danny took the mobile from the guard and tapped in some numbers. He brought it up to his ear before flinging it across the deck of the ferry, grabbing my hand and shouting, "Go!"

We dodged seats, bags and people's legs and crashed through the ferry doors on to the outdoor deck.

"We're nearly in the middle!"

"We're going to be in so much trouble if we don't time-shift," Danny shouted as we clambered on to the railings of the ferry.

I held his hand. "You ready?"

"Don't!" the guard yelled.

"One, two, three..."

And we jumped.

Chapter Twenty-Seven

The Thames in 2016 was as clean as the water in a swimming pool compared to the filthy river in 1730. I gasped for air the second I emerged from the murky water. Fat drops of rain splashed on my face. It was daytime but the sky was overcast with black clouds. I fought against the current and thrashed around looking for Danny. Barges and boats were criss-crossing the Thames and I was right in the middle. How would I manage to swim to the north bank without being squished by a barge? I tried to calm my breathing but panic set in every time water sloshed into my mouth.

"Maisie!"

Danny was behind me holding on to a broken barrel, furiously kicking against the current. I let myself drift to him and grabbed the slats of wood.

"This water tastes disgusting." He grasped my hand and held on. "I got a mouthful of it on my way up."

I'd choked on a mouthful too and now my teeth were chattering because the water was so cold. "We need to get to land."

Danny nodded and we both started kicking and paddling our broken barrel towards the city, but I could feel the strength of the water against us. Rain distorted my view, but a rebuilt London, sixty-four years after the fire, sprawled in front of us, a grey, miserable mass of buildings clinging to the north bank. My whole body shuddered with cold and I so wished it was summer.

The smell of fish mixed with a stench like dirty toilets clung to my nostrils. I didn't want to breathe the stink in but it was a struggle to push myself through the water without taking massive gulps of air.

"Hold up!" a voice boomed behind us. "There're children out there."

Still clutching the barrel, Danny and I flipped on to our backs. A stocky weather-beaten man stood on the edge of a boat filled with wooden barrels, like the one we had hold of except intact. A boy on the boat handed him a coil of rope and the man chucked one end towards us. The rope smacked the water and we kicked our way towards it, grabbed it and let the man pull us in. It was a struggle to climb up the high side of the boat but strong hands under my armpits yanked me up and over to safety. I sprawled out on the wooden deck and got my breath back as rain pounded down.

"How did you end up in the drink?" the man asked.

Danny coughed and spat out some water. "We fell off a boat."

The man raised an eyebrow and it was obvious he didn't believe us. We were telling the truth: we had fallen, well jumped, except the boat was in 2016 not 1730.

The man tapped the side of his nose with a

dirty finger. "Stowaways, eh? We can drop you along with our goods at Billingsgate. Then you be on your way."

We both nodded. "Thank you very much," I managed to say before my teeth started chattering again.

The man grunted a reply and threw us a blanket. We huddled beneath it, our backs against one of the barrels, trying to warm ourselves as the rain splattered down and the boat rocked and swayed its way across the Thames towards the city.

Billingsgate was swarming with men unloading goods from boats moored along the bank. A couple of older boys started to roll the barrels off the boat. The man who'd rescued us tipped his cap as we followed the boys and the barrels on to firm ground. We unclipped the soaking wet cloaks that our future selves had given us and threw them around our shoulders. Now all we had to do was find twenty-four Trinity Lane and Lizzie.

London stank. I could only manage tiny breaths without gagging. I guess smoke, tar and burning buildings had masked the stink of London in 1666. But now... A woman emptied a chamber pot into the street from an upstairs window. The cobbles were filthy with a wet film of slime and dung covering them. Drains either side ran with rainwater, piss from the pots and lumps of human poo. It made me gag. Danny grabbed my arm, and as I stopped and turned to him, he burped and was sick straight on to the cobbles.

I wanted to be anywhere but here. The middle of the fire of London was better than this. I couldn't imagine how Lizzie was coping. Maybe she wasn't.

Rats splashed through the gunk in the gutters and swarmed over what was left of a dead cat. I pulled Danny out of the rain and into the shadow of an overhang of an upper storey of a house. "Do we even know where we are?"

Danny took the laminated map from his trouser pocket. "We followed this road up from Billingsgate on to Thames Street. We need to keep going straight until we pass a church called St Martin's, and Trinity Lane should be third on the right."

"I didn't think anything could be worse than what we've already been through."

Danny was pale and looked like he'd be sick again any second. "Maybe this is a smell you get used to after time. Like your farm."

"I can't believe you're comparing our farm again to this stink. Our pigs smell sweet compared to this."

Wrapping our cloaks around us and pulling the hoods up, we set off again, splashing through the wet, dirty streets. Even though it was cold and wet the streets were busy with men and women rushing from shop to shop, and people bartering on the street corners and selling roasted chestnuts.

"Trinity Lane!" I said, pointing to the sign on

the corner house opposite us.

Number twenty-four was towards the end of a decent looking street of three-storey townhouses. The road was still filthy and swimming with muck but the houses themselves seemed well cared for and we passed a dressmaker and cobbler's shop. I took a deep breath and knocked on the door. There was no sound from inside and no candlelight flickering in the window like there was in other houses in the street. I knocked again.

"There isn't anyone there," a woman called across from the doorway of the house opposite. "They're always away travelling, 'on business' or so they say." She smoothed down the full skirt of her pale blue dress and studied us.

I had the key to the door in the locket round my neck but I wasn't comfortable opening the door with the woman watching. I played with the locket, unsure what to do. I banged harder on the door.

"There was a girl here earlier in the week, about your age," the lady said, pulling on long cream gloves. "But she left. I'd never seen her before. She said she was a cousin of Daniel's."

Danny and I glanced at each other. "She left? Do you know where she went?"

The lady shook her head. "She didn't say. Kept herself to herself." She nodded a goodbye just as a horse and carriage pulled up in front of her house.

"I hope she's wrong." I took the key out of the locket and turned it in the lock. It took a moment for our eyes to adjust to the gloom of the hallway.

I closed the front door behind us, shutting out the rain.

"Lizzie?" I shouted from the bottom of the stairs. Nothing. All I could hear was the constant drum of rain outside. I lifted my sodden cloak from off the floorboards and clattered up the wooden stairs to the first floor.

"She's definitely not here," Danny said, following me to the first-floor landing. "She's stupid enough to have gone off on her own."

"And if she has we have to go after her."

"We can't look for her unless we know where she's gone."

The house was like a time machine. It must have been built sometime after the Great Fire of London but it was filled with items and furniture from all periods of history. The ground floor was mainly used for storage and had enough boxes of food, medical supplies and toiletries to last a lifetime. I hoped we wouldn't need them. There were bars at the windows and multiple locks on the front and back doors.

The first floor was where they lived. The large front room overlooked the street and had armchairs arranged around the fireplace, a rug covering the floorboards and shutters at the windows. The fireplace was set, ready to be lit. It was cold inside with the rain still hammering the windowpanes.

Danny closed the shutters. "It's getting dark already."

I reached for the box of matches on the

mantelpiece and noticed a piece of paper tucked behind one of the candlesticks. I unfolded it and read it aloud.

Maisie & Danny

I can't wait for you any longer. It's been 6 days since M, L & D were here & they promised me they were going straight to you and would make sure you found me as soon as possible. 6 days! I'm scared. I think someone's watching the house. Maybe you're not even coming to get me and I'm wasting my time leaving this note for you. I'm going to the cottage on the other side of the river M, L & D told me about. I've drawn a map below of the route I'm going to take. We have to find each other.

Lizzie x

"I can't believe she's been here nearly a week," I said.

"I can't believe she's managed to survive on her own for that long."

"But how can it be six days since she saw our future selves?" I asked. "They'd only just left her here when they met us."

"Maybe we jumped in the Thames too late. Think about it. If time shifts from different places, 1471 in Warwick Castle, 1666 in Barnet, then maybe we jumped a few seconds too late and ended up in 1730 but a few days after Lizzie got here. Don't look so blank."

"My head's going to explode." I put Lizzie's note back on the mantelpiece. "So we lost her in the Thames in 1666, found out from our future selves in 2016 where Lizzie was and now we've gone and lost her again in 1730."

"That's pretty much it," Danny said.

Time really had become meaningless and yet it meant everything. It was like we were part of a Wii game and our older selves had the controls and were guiding us through the maze of time.

"Isn't it the oddest thing in the world talking about our future selves," I said. "I mean I had a conversation with myself. Except it's me and not me at the same time. It's like talking to yourself but with someone whose experiences we've not had yet, which makes our future selves different from how we are now. Does that make any sense?"

"I think you've had way too much time to think about things."

I picked up the letter again. "Do you think it was someone from the future watching the house?"

"It's probably no one, she's just being paranoid." Danny shivered. "Let's light this fire." He took the matches and lit the kindling beneath the logs. The fire spat and crackled and smoked but took hold.

I wanted to sink into the armchair nearest the fire, close my eyes and pretend I was in our living room at home with Benji asleep on the rug at my feet. I longed to smell a roast dinner cooking and hear Mum clanging pots and pans about in the kitchen.

Danny stoked the fire and warmth began to filter into the room. I realised we were still in our wet clothes and dripping water on to the floor. I started to giggle.

Danny looked up from the fireplace. "What's so funny?"

"Everything. We look ridiculous. Lizzie's gone missing again and it's 1730. Less than two hours ago it was 2016."

"I'm glad you're finding it funny." He stepped away from the fireplace as flames leapt high. "I was just thinking that if Lizzie hadn't stood up on the boat and fallen in we'd be home by now."

"We don't know that."

"Don't keep defending her."

"I'm not." We stared at each other. Danny's hair was flattened to his forehead and his thick sodden cloak was making a puddle of water on the floor. "Our future selves work as a team – we need to work together too if we want to make it home."

Danny smiled. "Your hair looks funny."

~

We heated baked beans in a pot over the fire and toasted bread on a fork. We ate it cross-legged on the rug. We decided we would stay the night and leave early in the morning as there was no point in going after Lizzie at night and in torrential rain.

"I hope you're right about Lizzie being paranoid. I mean she was on her own, in a strange house, stuck in the past, surely that would make anyone, especially Lizzie, start imagining things?"

"Of course I'm right," Danny said, putting his empty bowl on the floor and resting back on the rug.

"And maybe people are watching, like the woman across the street. We hardly look or behave like eighteenth-century children."

The wind howled outside and rattled the windowpanes and the rain's rhythmic thud made me glad to be inside.

"It's worrying me," Danny said. "Why our future selves didn't come with us. Where do they go and what are they doing?"

"They're protecting us. They said they had stuff to deal with."

"Yeah, bad stuff."

"You don't know that." But I was worried about them, which meant I was worried about us.

~

I had a bath. Not a proper twenty-first-century bath with hot water from a tap and bubble bath, but it was a bath all the same, in a tin tub with hot water heated over the fire. There was a choice of eighteenth-century clothes in one of the rooms on the top floor. I chose a plain bluish-green shimmering dress that was too big for me but was at least clean and warm and suitable for 1730.

On the second floor were three bedrooms belonging to each of us. The bed in Lizzie's room was unmade and clothes lay scattered over the floor and the wardrobe doors were left open. She seemed to have left in a hurry. Danny's room was next to Lizzie's at the back of the house and despite being furnished in an eighteenth-century style it was filled with battery-operated gadgets. My room felt familiar as if it belonged to me, which I guess it did. It was filled with things gathered from all periods of time, the old alongside the new. The window overlooked the street and I shivered as I closed the shutters on rain-soaked London. I thumbed through the novels stacked on the windowsill and noticed there were books by one of Mum's favourite authors. I picked up a book with a cover I didn't recognise and realised why when I saw the year it was published: 2018.

I opened the top drawer of the chest and gasped. Lying on top of jumpers and T-shirts was a photo. It was of Mum and Dad standing outside our farmhouse with Ollie, but he was older, an adult, taller than Dad and he looked like he'd been working out at a gym. This was the future if we didn't find our way home in time. Mum's, Dad's and Ollie's future without me. And mine without them. I put the photo back. My future self needed it but I didn't because we were going to get home.

Chapter Twenty-Eight

Thud, thud, thud. I scrambled out of bed. It was completely dark and I couldn't even see where the door was.

"Maisie!" Danny hissed. The door creaked open and Danny's face appeared, lit by the candle he held.

"It's the middle of the night, Danny," I said, yawning.

"Come with me." He took my hand and led me on to the landing. He blew the candle out and pushed his bedroom door open.

"But..."

"Shush," he said, and guided me across his room to the window. "Lizzie wasn't being paranoid." He pointed to the top window of the house opposite. A man, dimly lit by candlelight, peered out of the window.

"What does that prove?" I asked.

Danny pulled me below the window so we were out of sight. "He's got binoculars. That's not very eighteenth-century is it."

"Are you sure?"

"Positive," he said. "I think we should leave right now."

"It's the middle of the night and still raining out there." The truth was it was warm and cosy in the safe house and I felt just that – safe. I'd had a few hours' sleep in a proper bed for only the third time in over a week and I didn't want to give that up, but I knew there was no choice – we couldn't stay here forever.

Danny gathered his belongings together. "No wonder Lizzie freaked out."

We dressed in warm clothes, dry cloaks and packed a change of modern clothes in the hope of eventually time-shifting to 2016 and then home to 2012. We crept downstairs and gathered together money, food, matches and a compass, and split the stuff between two bags that we slung across our shoulders. I put Lizzie's letter in my cloak pocket and made sure future Lizzie's key and locket were still safely round my neck. We checked the London map against Lizzie's drawing and decided on our route before we left.

Shutting the door to the safe house felt like abandoning the last link to home and our future selves. Where were they? Did they even know what was happening? I pulled the hood of my cloak over my head and with Danny next to me we stepped into the street. The rain pounded down, soaking us instantly with fat drops of cold water. Lanterns above the doorways dimly lit the streets. We splashed along the middle of the road, away from the filth flowing along the gutters on each side.

"Do you think anyone's following?" I asked as we turned the corner and left Trinity Lane behind.

"They're being careful not to be spotted if they are."

We kept a fast pace, practically jogging along Thames Street. My heart thudded at the thought of who might be waiting for us in the dark corners of these eerie London streets. Despite the darkness and rain we weren't the only ones about. We passed a couple of men cursing as they stumbled away from the closed door of a tavern. They were too drunk to bother us and we slipped past them. Stray dogs stalked the empty streets, their howls echoing after us. In the doorway of a house near the river a bundle of rags stirred and a rain-soaked, bony-faced woman made us jump. We didn't stop until we reached London Bridge. We huddled together, sheltering beneath the gables of the house on the corner of the bridge and caught our breath. I looked back the way we'd come, at the rain-drenched street, but couldn't make out anyone following us.

"Hopefully he hasn't even realised we've gone," I said, imagining the man still at the window in the relative warmth of the house instead of outside in the freezing winter rain. I shivered but there was no way to warm up or even begin to dry out until we reached the cottage.

"Can you even believe we saw the houses on this bridge go up in flames less than a day ago," Danny said, as we started to walk across.

"At least this is easier than rowing across that." I pointed to the glassy blackness of the Thames and shuddered.

"It's just as wet though."

Our feet sloshed through the water running

over the cobbles. The bridge seemed narrower than it looked from the river with the three-storey houses towering above us on both sides.

"It feels like we're going in circles," I said. "Chasing Lizzie through time, ending back here in the same place but in a different century. I wonder where Lizzie thinks we are?"

"She probably thinks we abandoned her. We're so going to get grief about that when we do find her."

"She was the one who fell off the boat."

"Ha! At last, you're not defending her."

"I'm just stating the truth. No one's to blame."

Danny sighed and we walked on in silence. We were leaving London behind for the second time. I was soaked through and so cold my teeth chattered, the only sound apart from the continuous rain. My cloak and eighteenth-century clothes felt like weights hanging off my shoulders. I really wanted to be at home in front of the open fire in our living room wearing my snuggly fleece top, jogging trousers and big warm fluffy socks. I kept thinking of the photo I'd found in my future self's room, of Mum, Dad and a grown-up Ollie outside our farmhouse without me.

Danny stopped and grabbed my arm. We were in the middle of the bridge.

"What?" I asked.

"Listen." He swung round to face the way we'd come.

I peered into the darkness and saw grey shadows at the other end of the bridge. "Riders!" I said. The thud of hooves was masked by the thunder of rain on the bridge.

"Maybe it's us?" Danny asked.

"And if it's not?"

There was nowhere to hide, so we ran, away from London and whoever it was behind us. But we weren't fast enough. Two riders on grey horses thundered past us and cut off our escape route. We turned back towards London but they circled us. The horses snorted plumes of white breath into the icy air. Hoods obscured the faces of the two riders but I could tell they were both men although I wasn't sure if either of them was the man at the window.

Danny charged towards the nearest rider and threw his arms in the air. "What do you want with us?"

The horse reared and Danny dodged away from its kicking hooves. The man regained control of the horse and grabbed Danny by the hood of his cloak.

"What do we want with you?" the man said, leaning towards Danny and revealing the edge of a black tattoo on the side of his neck. "That you will find out in time. It's us that'll be asking the questions from now on." Clinging on tight to the horse with his legs, the man clasped the back of Danny's neck with his free hand.

"Ouch!" Danny yelled and pulled away.

The man released his grip on Danny. "Get her," he said to the other rider.

I closed my eyes and felt the cold rain pummel

my face. If only we'd managed to reach the other side of the bridge. There were dark crevices between the houses where we could have hidden from the riders. I could see the exact spot so clearly in my mind, and then the ground shuddered and, for just a second or two, I could no longer feel the rain on my face or even the cobbles beneath my feet.

I landed with a thud on squelchy ground and heard the rain again bouncing off something above my head. I opened my eyes. I was where I'd imagined, beneath the gables of one of the houses in the lane protected from the rain, with mud beneath my feet. My heart beat so fast and my hands trembled from more than just the cold. But most importantly I was on my own. Danny...

Hitching up my dress I ran as fast as I could through the torrential rain, mud splattering my legs as I covered the short distance between the lane and the main road. I stopped when I reached the end houses and looked along the bridge to where Danny was between the two riders, all of them still searching for me. "Danny!" I shouted as I ran towards them.

He turned and ran towards me, rainwater flying up around him. The riders spun their horses round but I reckoned we had a chance. I willed my legs to go faster. I'd nearly reached Danny. I closed my eyes, held my right hand out in front of me and pictured the inside of the cottage and the three beds with our names carved into the wood of the headboards. As Danny grabbed my hand I imagined tracing my fingers over the grooves of my name.

"What happened?" he shouted.

"Don't let go!" I kept the thought of my name carved in the wooden headboard of my bed and held on tightly to him. The rain stopped.

Chapter Twenty-Nine

This time my feet thudded on to floorboards, but I couldn't feel Danny's hand in mine. I opened my eyes to find I was alone, dripping water on to the floor next to my bed in the cottage.

The bedroom door slammed open and Lizzie charged in brandishing a frying pan. She stopped dead when she saw me. "How did you get in here?"

"I time-shifted," I said.

"From where?" Lizzie asked.

"From London Bridge."

"I mean from what year?"

"1730."

She frowned. "But that's like now. Where's Danny?"

I burst into tears. "I think I've lost him. I did what our future selves said was too risky to do and tried to time-shift us both here but only I've ended up here and I don't know where Danny is..."

"Maisie, slow down. I don't understand a word you're saying." She put the frying pan on the floor and made me sit down on the bed. "Start from the beginning. Where have you been for the last week?"

A sob caught in my throat and I swallowed hard and wiped away the tears streaming down my already wet face. "For us it's not even been twenty-four hours since you fell in the Thames."

"Well for me it's been a week. But forget about that. I want to know how you time-shifted here if you were already in 1730?"

I sniffed. "Me and Danny left the house on Trinity Lane in the middle of the night after we saw the man in the house opposite spying on us. We were on the bridge when two men on horses cut us off and grabbed Danny, and I... and I..."

"Time-shifted."

"Yeah, to the exact spot I was imagining in my head."

"Which was where?"

"Beneath the gables of a house in a lane on the south bank of the river. I ran back to the bridge, Danny saw me and legged it. The safest place that came into my head was this bedroom, and as soon as Danny grabbed my hand... boom, we time-shifted. Except it's only me that's here. I've lost Danny."

"When our future selves found me five days ago they said they were going to meet with you and tell you where I was," Lizzie said. "Before they left, Maisie explained a few things about her ability to time-shift to wherever and whenever she wants and also that I, well my future self, can time-shift too." She looked down and scuffed her feet on the floorboards. "With almost as much accuracy as you."

"And what about Danny?"

"I think that's the problem, that's why he

didn't make it here with you. Future Danny told me he can time-shift with either you or me but he doesn't always end up in the right place. He called time-shifting a gift."

"That's what you called it. Well not you exactly but future you," I said. "She found me in the attic of that lady's house during the fire and told me then that I had the ability to time-shift at will."

"And that's why those people in the wood and now on the bridge are hunting us, because of our ability to time-shift."

I stared at the puddle of water I was making on the floor. My hair was wet and plastered to my neck and I shivered.

"You need to get warm," Lizzie said.

I followed her out of the bedroom into the main living room, which was heated by a roaring fire. For the first time I noticed that Lizzie was wearing an oyster-coloured dress with a shawl covering her shoulders and her hair was clean and shiny. I removed my cloak and began to drip dry in front of the fire. "Something smells good." I pointed to the lidded pot hanging on a hook over the flames.

"Beef and vegetable casserole," Lizzie said. "I made it myself. I bought meat from the butcher on Thames Street and got vegetables from the garden."

I squeezed the water out of my hair. "So what happened after you fell off the boat?"

"I swallowed a lot of disgusting water. I mean a lot, and when I surfaced you two and the boat had gone, it was daylight and London wasn't on fire anymore."

"1730," I said.

"Except I didn't know that at the time. I seriously thought I was going to drown until this elderly man and his dog in this rickety old boat rescued me." She looked away from me and took a deep breath. "He took me home to his wife and they fussed over me, found me some clothes, gave me food and a bed for the night. I was really lucky that he found me and not some criminal."

"How did our future selves know where to find you?"

She shrugged. "I don't know. The next day when I was doing an errand for Mrs Tanner I literally came face to face with them in the street and they took me to the house in Trinity Lane. They said I had to stay in the house. I didn't even get a chance to thank Mr Tanner and his wife. What took you another five days?"

"It didn't," I said, holding my hands over the fire and rubbing them together. "We saw our future selves just after they'd left you; we were only another couple of hours at most until we reached the house. And you weren't there."

"This whole time-shifting thing is doing my head in; it's way too complicated."

"Actually, it's quite simple," I said, turning my back on the fire and facing her. "We may be stuck in time but you and me have the ability to time-shift to wherever and whenever we want, and Danny should be able to if he's with us."

"But he didn't time-shift with you."

"But he must be able to because our future selves all time-shift at will with no problem. Danny was with them when they met us in 2016, when they saved you in the wood in 1471 and when they saw you five days ago. So it's possible, and if it's possible it means we can time-shift home together."

"Just because you managed to time-shift at will, doesn't mean I can yet."

"Your future self told me to believe in ourselves." I went to the window and peered out. Rain streaked the glass and all I could see was darkness.

"Where do you think Danny is?" Lizzie asked.

"I don't know."

"Maybe he's still on the bridge. Maybe he didn't time-shift anywhere?"

"If that's true then the men who were after us have got him."

"There's only one way to find out." She took her cloak off the hook on the wall next to the front door and chucked a bowl of water on the fire. Flames hissed and spluttered and smoke engulfed the fireplace and the room darkened. Only the lantern on the table gave off any light. She handed me a dry cloak and took hold of my hand. "Let's time-shift to the bridge and see if he's still there."

"What if you don't time-shift and I end up losing you too?"

"What did my future self say, 'believe'?" She

tightened her grip on my hand. "So believe."

"Okay," I said. "Concentrate really hard on London Bridge and imagine that we're there."

We closed our eyes. I imagined the cold rain falling on my face, the cobbles beneath my feet and the three-storey houses on either side of the bridge towering over us. I squeezed Lizzie's hand to make sure she was still there. I concentrated so hard on the bridge yet I could still feel the warmth of the room and smell the casserole. I opened my eyes. Lizzie still had hers closed.

"It's not working," I said.

"I was only imagining the bridge from the river anyway," Lizzie said, opening her eyes. "I'd have ended up back in the water."

"I guess we'll have to walk there."

Lizzie's grip tightened on my hand.

"Ouch!" I said.

"I can hear something." She released my hand, went to the door and pressed her ear against it. All I could hear was the rain drumming on the window.

Lizzie spun round to face me. "I can hear horses."

"We're so stupid; if those men knew of the Trinity Lane safe house, then why wouldn't they know about this one?" I said. "We need to get out of here. We can hide in the wood."

"Yeah, because that worked so well last time," Lizzie said.

Thud. Someone's full weight crashed into the cottage door. Dust puffed from the sides. Lizzie backed away and I pulled her into the bedroom and closed the door. There was no lock and the only way out was through the window. I grabbed a blanket from the bed and wrapped it around my hand before smashing the glass. There was another thud on the cottage door and the sound of wood splintering.

"Maisie, hurry!"

I wiped away the shards of glass. "You first."

I pushed Lizzie towards the window. Something flashed in front of me and floorboards creaked as feet landed on them and then I was staring face to face with my future self.

"Maisie?" we both said together.

"Just in time," future Lizzie said, releasing her hand from Maisie's and moving over to the bedroom door. Future Danny did the same. There was a huge crash as the cottage door gave way.

Maisie took hold of my hand. "There's not much time. You two need to get out of here."

"But I've lost Danny, if he's with them…"

"He's not. He time-shifted on the bridge."

"To where?"

"1940. You need to get Danny back, so get to the bridge. We'll meet you there. Go!"

Lizzie scrambled through the window, catching her dress and tearing it as she dropped on to the ground on the other side. The bedroom door flew open and I caught sight of one of the men from the bridge just as future Maisie, Lizzie and Danny charged towards him knocking him back into the main room of the cottage. Wrapping my cloak around me, I climbed out of the window and landed in the mud. Rain splattered down. Banging, shouts and thuds echoed from inside the cottage and then everything went silent.

Chapter Thirty

"They've time-shifted, haven't they?" Lizzie said through chattering teeth.

"I think so."

Lizzie's hair was already wet and plastered to her neck. She threw her hood over her head and wrapped her cloak tighter round her.

"Let's get their horses," I said.

"Uh uh, not again."

We picked our way in the dark through the long grass to the front of the cottage. In the faint light spilling from the broken down front door I could just make out the grey shadows of the two horses. The horse nearest the cottage neighed as I caught hold of its reins.

"They're big horses," Lizzie said, standing well back.

"Tell you what," I said, putting my left foot in the stirrup and heaving myself into the saddle and bundling up the mass of cloak and dress material away from my feet. "Get up behind me."

The horse was strong and larger than any I'd ridden before. I managed to rein him over to the stack of logs next to the front door. Lizzie stood on them and clambered up behind me. The horse snorted and pounded the ground. I held on tightly to the reins and Lizzie gripped me around my waist. I could feel her shivering. I gently kicked the horse and we shot off, racing through the rain with water and mud flying up around us. Lizzie tightened her grip until it felt like she was squeezing my insides out.

~

London Bridge was empty.

"He definitely time-shifted then," Lizzie said, scrambling down off the horse. "I'm so never getting on a horse again."

I dismounted, patted the horse's neck, let go of the reins and watched it canter back the way we'd come. "When we get back home you could come over to our farm and learn to ride my pony."

"Maisie, I'm never going to like riding," she said, pulling her cloak tight around her. "But I'd like to see your farm."

We huddled out of the rain beneath the overhang of the end building on the bridge.

"What now?" Lizzie asked.

"We wait for our future selves to turn up."

"They'd better not be long, I'm freezing."

My teeth chattered and I shivered because my clothes were wet and sticking to my skin. The rain lashed down sending a river of water running along the bridge and into the gutter.

"Did you notice I have tattoos," Lizzie said. "Mum will kill me."

"Lizzie you do realise *you* don't actually have tattoos, it's your future self that does."

"Yeah but I'll have them in the future."

"Only if you choose to have them."

"I think I look cool, you know, older."

"You looking for someone?" a raspy voice

suddenly said. Lizzie grasped my arm as an old woman staggered out of the shadows opposite us. She clutched a bottle in her hand and swayed as she moved towards us.

I stepped forward. "Yeah, we're looking for our friend, a boy..."

"A boy. A boy you say." She waved the bottle at us. "I saw a boy here, a little while ago, a boy and a girl 'bout your age, and two men on horses. The boy and girl disappeared. I swear they just disappeared." She started to laugh and then erupted into a hacking cough.

Lizzie leant towards me. "That was you and Danny."

"I know, I don't think she realises though."

"That's because she's too drunk."

The woman finished coughing and spat a big blob of green phlegm on to the cobbles.

"Yuck," Lizzie said.

I swallowed back the sick feeling in my throat. "Are you sure you didn't just imagine this boy and girl 'disappear'. It doesn't exactly sound possible."

"I knows what I saw."

"I bet you often see things when you've been drinking."

"This ain't strong stuff." She held out the bottle and chuckled. "Tastes of watered down piss anyways."

"Did anyone else see what you saw?"

She shook her head and her wet grey hair slapped her face and remained stuck. "There ain't no one about but me," she said and started coughing again.

A low rumble like thunder and a loud splash made me turn to look along the bridge in time to see future Maisie, Danny and Lizzie walking towards us.

"She bothering you?" future Danny asked when they reached us.

"No. But she said she saw a boy and girl disappear," I said, pointing at myself.

"Is that so?" He turned to the woman and she took a step back. "A figment of your imagination, that's all."

She staggered away from us towards the houses and inns of Southwark. "A lot of strange people abroad tonight!" she called out.

"Now's really not the time to be making friends," future Danny said.

Lizzie frowned. "We were hardly making friends."

"He's only teasing you," future Lizzie said, and ruffled his hair. "Get used to it."

"Where did you take them? The two men?" I asked.

"To a place they won't be a nuisance," Maisie said.

"Where's that?"

Maisie smiled. "An empty cell in 1625 at The Clink, a prison on Bankside. They won't be bothering us for a while."

"So how do we find Danny?" I asked.

"He's in 1940s London," future Lizzie said. "So we're going to time-shift there and find him."

"You're coming with us?" Lizzie asked.

"Of course," Maisie said. "We really can't risk anything else happening to you." We stood in a circle and held hands, Lizzie between her and my future self and me holding on to future Lizzie and future Danny.

"How can we shift to a time and place we've never been to?" Lizzie asked.

"You've always wanted to be an actor," future Danny said. "Well imagine you're in a film, set in World War II. Close your eyes. And you Maisie. Imagine the sound of German fighter planes overhead, dropping bombs on south London. We're in a terraced street in Southwark and it's dark and hot, it smells of smoke and burning buildings."

I took one last look across the 1730s Thames at London and closed my eyes. I tried to forget about the rain falling on my face and how cold and shivery I was in my wet clothes. Instead I concentrated on believing I was hot, dry and breathing rancid smoke into my lungs. I imagined what it would be like to hear explosions and see the underbelly of fighter planes releasing deadly bombs above a dark city. Future Danny's grip tightened on my hand.

The rain stopped and for a moment it felt like I was flying, my feet touching nothing but air before landing back on solid ground with a jolt. The drum of rain was replaced with the wail of an air-raid siren. I opened my eyes. It was pitch-black but hot and we were in the middle of an empty terraced street. There were no streetlights or any lights shining from the houses.

"We did it, we time-shifted," Lizzie said.

"Do you know where we are, Danny?" future Lizzie asked, as the five of us released hands.

He nodded. "My usual place in Southwark."

"Your usual place?" I asked.

"I end up here a lot when I don't time-shift properly with Maisie and Lizzie. I was stuck here for eleven months the first time before these two found me again."

"Seriously?" Lizzie said.

"And how did they find you?" I asked.

Danny glanced at my future self and she nodded. He put his hand on my shoulder. "Nearly a year after I disappeared, you discovered that not only could you time-shift to anywhere in the past, present and future, but you had the ability to see where a person was in time and then time-shift to where that person was. You nearly scared me to death time-shifting right in front of me in the street. Luckily there was no one else around to witness it."

"So," Lizzie said slowly. "You're saying if Maisie thinks about a person, she can time-shift to exactly where they are?"

My future self nodded. "I have to concentrate on that person, I mean really concentrate on them, but yes, I get an image of where that person is and then, if I want to, I can time-shift to exactly where they are, whatever place or period in time they may be."

"Which is how you found Lizzie in 1730 and us in the cottage before," I said.

"And me and Danny can't do that?" Lizzie asked.

"As far as we know," future Lizzie said. "Maisie is the *only* person who can time-shift to where another person is at any given time."

"That's the reason why these people from the future want us so badly?" I asked.

"You got it," future Lizzie said.

"Come on," future Danny said. "We can talk more once we're indoors."

The air-raid siren continued to wail and Danny beckoned for us to follow him. We jogged after him through the maze of tightly packed terraced streets, finally stopping in front of an end terrace with a shiny number one on its black front door. Danny unlocked it using the key on the chain around his neck.

The house was oddly familiar. It was like stepping into the hallway of my grandma's terraced house in Caerphilly. We followed future Danny into the front room. He switched on the tall lamp in the corner and the familiarity with Grandma's house ended. There were blackout blinds up at the front windows and a wireless radio on the sideboard.

"Welcome to my World War II home," future Danny said. He flopped down in the armchair next to the fireplace. "I've spent quite a lot of time here."

"Shouldn't we get in an underground bunker

or something?" Lizzie asked.

"Don't worry, this house survives the Blitz," future Danny said. "After ending up in 1940 for the fifth time and realising it was becoming a regular occurrence, I researched World War II and the Blitz and found which streets survived the bombings. The next time I ended up back here, I bought this place."

Maisie held a finger to her lips and moved to the window. "Listen."

We fell silent. I could just make out the drone of a plane overhead.

Future Lizzie went over to the wireless and turned the button at the front. There was a crackling noise that continued as she kept turning the knob. She paused when a male voice could be heard but the crackle made it impossible to understand what was being said.

And then the first bomb dropped.

Chapter Thirty-One

It was a huge explosion – a roar followed by a massive bang that sounded like it was in the next street and hurt my ears and made the windows rattle. All of us apart from future Danny ducked. "Forget about the wireless, Lizzie," he said calmly from the armchair. "If that bomb landed where I think it did then it's the 7th September 1940."

"Are you sure it's safe here?" Lizzie asked.

"Absolutely positive," future Danny said. "Us being here isn't going to change where the Germans dropped their bombs."

"If you say so," Lizzie said and moved away from the window.

There was another explosion and another but they sounded further away and didn't make the windows rattle. I couldn't begin to understand how scary it would be actually living in 1940 and not knowing if a bomb would hit your house.

"Sit down you two," future Danny said, pointing towards the empty armchairs. "We're going to be here a while."

I sat in the armchair opposite him and Lizzie flopped down in the middle chair.

"I'm going to cook some dinner," my future self said. "You coming Lizzie?"

Lizzie scrambled back up from the chair. Future Lizzie laughed and put her hand on

Lizzie's shoulder. "She meant me, not you."

Lizzie sighed and sank back down. "It's way too confusing."

"Tell me about it," future Danny said. "I'm here and yet not here, get your head round that."

"You're going to give them a headache," future Lizzie said as she left the room.

I turned to future Danny. "So where do you think Danny is?"

"I presume he'll have done the same thing I did when I first time-shifted here, and went and found Grandad's house."

"His grandad's?" Lizzie asked.

"Of course," I said. "Danny's grandad grew up in London until he was evacuated during the war. He's always telling us about it."

"And in September 1940 he's eight years old and still living in London, a few streets away from here," future Danny said. "He hasn't been evacuated yet."

"Have you met him?" I asked.

"Many, many times. My great grandfather took me in when I first time-shifted here. I'm pretty much part of the family. Literally."

~

There were only two bedrooms upstairs. The back room had a double bed, dressing table and wardrobe and we got to pick through the choice of 1940s clothes, which were all too big but way better than the cold, dirty and wet eighteenth-century dresses we were shivering in.

"Ah, finally, something semi-comfortable," Lizzie said, pulling on a knee-length grey skirt and tightening the belt. She did up the buttons of a white blouse.

I looked in the dressing table mirror and tied my mass of curls into a messy ponytail. I wore black trousers with the bottoms rolled up and a thin short-sleeved jumper.

"I can't believe you have the ability to time-shift to where anybody is," Lizzie said.

"My future self has the ability. I'm sure I don't yet."

"But it's amazing. You could think about your Mum and time-shift to wherever she is. Or someone famous. Eek! Just imagine time-shifting to where Robert Pattinson is right now." She joined me in front of the mirror and began to brush her hair. "We look so different from when we first time-shifted."

"We're looking more and more like our future selves."

~

A spicy tomato smell drifted up the stairs from the kitchen and my stomach rumbled. The beans on toast I'd had with Danny in the Trinity Lane house seemed a very long time ago. Future Danny and Lizzie sat at the kitchen table while Maisie stirred something in a large pan on the stove. Blackout blinds covered the window and the glass in the back door.

"That smells so good," I said as we joined them at the table.

"You're a great cook," future Lizzie said to me. "At least you will be. You can turn even the most basic of ingredients into something tasty."

Maisie ladled steaming food into five bowls and brought them to the table. "Butter bean and chorizo stew with roast potatoes."

We ate in silence, enjoying the warm smoky flavour of the stew. I crunched into a roast potato. "They're just like Mum makes them."

Future Danny glanced at Maisie and I realised too late what I'd said. I'd only eaten Mum's roast potatoes two weeks ago but for my future self it had been years. "I'm sorry, I didn't mean to..."

"It's okay, Maisie," she said, placing her spoon in her bowl. "I know they taste like Mum's. I want them to. A little piece of home, you know. I miss Mum, Dad and Ollie like crazy. All three of us miss home."

"If you get us home, back to the castle when we first time-shifted," Lizzie said, "what happens to you?"

"Our job is done," Maisie said.

"Yeah, I know that," Lizzie said. "But what *actually* happens to you?"

"We'll cease to exist," Danny said. "Because we are you and if you get back to Warwick Castle 21st March 2012, then in theory everything that has happened to us from that point onwards won't have the chance to happen. The future we made will no longer exist and you'll be free to live our lives."

"But," Lizzie said, scrunching her face up. "Us sitting here now talking to you is actually happening, right? So how can us getting back to the castle cancel all this out? It's already happened."

"Lizzie, we're brilliant," future Lizzie said, scraping her chair back and standing up. "Danny's theory is full of holes. I think if someone, say you, Maisie, after you get home, shifted to a point in time we'd been to or lived through, then you'd meet us, because like Lizzie said, we've already had this experience and nothing can change that."

"You're both so wrong," future Danny said, ruffling future Lizzie's hair and pulling her to him. He put his arm around her waist. I was glad Danny wasn't here to see how friendly they'd become.

I looked at Maisie. "What do you think?"

She stretched her hands out on the table and twisted the silver ring on her right thumb. "I think the notion of time and time shifting is by no means a straightforward thing," she said slowly. "As for what happens to the three of us when the three of you get home, only time will tell and maybe one day you'll find out."

"You mean if we time-shift again?" I said.

She nodded. "Our ability to time-shift isn't going to go away because you get back home. You're going to have to be really careful. Particularly you, Maisie."

"Don't go scaring them," future Lizzie said, pulling away from future Danny. She stacked the empty bowls together, went to the sink and turned on the tap.

"And what about the people chasing us?"

Lizzie said. "If you cease to exist and we still have the ability to time-shift aren't they going to keep coming after us?"

No one said a word. Future Danny looked across the table at Maisie. Future Lizzie turned off the tap and leant on the edge of the sink with her back to us.

"So we're not even going to be safe at home?" I asked.

"You'll be safer at home than you will be wandering through time on your own and exposed like this," Maisie said.

"Safer but not totally safe," I said.

"For years we've kept a relatively low profile, taking our time in planning how to get you home," future Danny said. "But recently we've all been time-shifting too much and they're on to us big time."

"Did Robbie tell those people who chased us in the wood where we were?" Lizzie asked.

"Robbie's a good guy," future Lizzie said. "He time-shifts by accident, he's not working for anyone and he's not on anyone's wanted list. He genuinely tried to help us. The Dunstable inn owners, however, were being paid for information about who Robbie sent to them. The man and woman who chased you to the wood in 1471 are convicts from the twenty-second century. They were given the choice of living in the past and hunting time shifters instead of a jail sentence. There are plenty of desperate people in the future willing to live in the past and capture time shifters like us. Like Billy the Kid in the wild west, there's a bounty on our heads."

"So, if the safest place to be is home, why aren't we going to get Danny now?" I asked.

"Patience, Maisie, you sound like Lizzie," future Danny said. "We'll wait for the all-clear and then go and get him. It'll be daylight in a few hours."

"You could try and get some sleep," Maisie said.

"What, with all the bombs going off?" Lizzie said.

"Maisie was only making a suggestion," future Lizzie said. "You could play a game. Danny, haven't you got a Gameboy or something?"

A high-pitched beep, beep, beep sounded out in the hallway. Future Danny dropped his mug on the table splashing coffee over the wood.

"What's that?" I asked

"The alarm," he said. "Someone's in the garden."

"Someone, as in the people chasing us?" Lizzie asked.

Future Danny nodded. "We need to get out of here now." He motioned for us all to stand up before dragging the kitchen table away from the window and pulling back the threadbare rug to reveal a trapdoor. "I was hoping we'd never need to use this."

Maisie put her hand on future Danny's shoulder. "Get them away from here," she said. "Go find Danny and we'll stall them."

Future Danny faltered then nodded. "We'll meet you on Blackfriars Road. Be careful."

Chapter Thirty-Two

We followed Danny through the trapdoor and down the narrow steps into the dark cellar. It smelt damp and musty. He switched on a torch and the beam of light revealed shelves next to the stairs filled with stuff. He shone the light back up the steps to future Lizzie as she closed the trapdoor. I heard them drag the table back into place.

"We're just going to wait down here and hope they won't find us?" Lizzie said.

Future Danny shone his torch across the cellar to a hole in the wall and what looked like a tunnel. "No, Lizzie, I'm smarter than that. Our escape route." He grabbed a rucksack off the shelf and swung it on his back before handing us a torch each. "Follow me and mind your heads."

The tunnel was wide enough but even Lizzie had to stoop as we walked along it. We hadn't gone far when we reached a padlocked door. "The air-raid shelter at the bottom of the garden," future Danny said as he opened it.

The shelter was cramped, hot and empty.

"It stinks," Lizzie said.

"You dug that tunnel yourself?" I asked future Danny as he unlocked the padlock on the door of the shelter.

"I had a lot of time on my hands when I was stuck here. I pretended I was Andy Dufresne digging my way to freedom."

"Who?" Lizzie asked.

"When you're old enough, watch *The Shawshank Redemption*. Then you'll understand." He dropped the padlock on the floor of the shelter. "Switch the torches off. And be ready to run." He scraped the door open. Immediately outside was a crumbling garden wall. Future Danny scrambled over it and glanced back towards the house. "Come on, keep your heads down."

I followed Lizzie over the wall, catching and ripping the edge of my jumper on the broken bricks. A thin strip of weed-filled wasteland ran the length of the terraces between the gardens. I looked back to the house. "It seems very quiet, Danny?" I whispered.

"They've time-shifted them away," he said, his voice faltering.

The night air was hot and smelt of smoke and reminded me of us running through the burning streets of London in 1666. The blackout was still in place, except where the bombs had hit, fires lit the night sky. I could hear distant rumbles of more bombs being dropped. We followed future Danny through the undergrowth. The terraced houses on either side of us were intact but I could see a glow lighting up the sky and hear a fire raging only streets away from us, probably from the bomb that had made the windows rattle.

One by one we squeezed through the fence at the end of the terrace on to a pavement. The street was empty with doors shut and windows blacked out, but I could hear shouts and a rumble of an engine not far away. In the distance, aeroplanes droned and bombs whistled then boomed as they exploded into something solid.

"It's so dark," I said. "How do the Germans know where to aim?"

"They just follow the Thames," future Danny said. "It's a clear night. In the moonlight the Thames shows up like a finger pointing straight to the centre of London. We need to get a move on; they haven't finished bombing this side of the river yet."

Our legs raced along the pavements as we followed future Danny along terraced streets that all looked identical until we reached the end of the street that had been bombed. The middle houses were missing on both sides, just smoking shells remained, their bricks, floorboards and furniture spewed out into the street. A fire ate away at what was left of the houses on the left side of the street and firefighters standing on the rubble hosed jets of water into the middle of the flames. Unlike the stillness of the other roads where I imagined people to be hiding in their basements or air-raid shelters, the neighbours were all in the street, comforting each other, sifting through rubble, searching for survivors... I shuddered and caught sight of a little girl crying and clutching a teddy bear as a woman knelt in front of her.

"Maisie, there's nothing we can do, it's already happened," future Danny said, putting his hand on my shoulder and turning me away from the devastation.

Danny's grandad's house was only a couple of roads away from where the bomb had dropped. Future Danny made us stop at the corner of the road.

"They so could have been bombed," I said.

Future Danny nodded. "It was a near miss. Grandad was evacuated not long after because of tonight's bombings."

"Which house is it?" I asked.

"Number twelve." He pulled binoculars out of his rucksack and studied the street.

"What's the plan?" Lizzie asked.

"We're going to go and knock on the door and ask for Danny."

"Seriously, that's the plan?" She raised an eyebrow.

Future Danny laughed. "This isn't an undercover operation. There's no need for us to be sneaking around or breaking in. That's my family in there, they're good people. They took me in when I first time-shifted here, they'll have done the same with Danny now. I can't see anyone watching the house. Come on. Just let me do the talking."

We crossed the road and stood outside number twelve. I couldn't believe this was actually Danny's grandad's house and his family were inside.

Future Danny knocked on the door. The noise and shouts from the bombed-out street nearby must have kept everyone awake. I listened for any movement inside the house – footsteps in the hallway and the door opened. A middle-aged man with grey hair, wearing trousers and a shirt with the sleeves rolled up, stared at us. "What on earth are you doing out in the street?" he said, glancing from future Danny to Lizzie and me.

"We're looking for our cousin Danny, someone said they'd seen a boy taken in here? He's twelve, with dark hair, he was wearing strange clothes, he'd been playing…"

"Yes, Danny's here," the man said.

"Alfred, who is it?" a woman's voice called from upstairs.

"Danny knocked on our door earlier, seemed a bit confused about where he was and how he got here. I was worried he'd suffered a knock to the head. He seemed to know my son but Will didn't know him."

"Maisie?" Danny, dressed in shorts and a jumper, appeared in the hallway behind Alfred and grinned. "You found me again then."

Alfred stepped back. "You'd better come in."

I ran inside and hugged Danny.

"We need to get Danny home," future Danny said from the doorstep. "His mother's worried to death about him, she was thinking the worst."

"You can't go out there now, it's not safe," Alfred said.

"Father, what's happening?" A boy appeared at the top of the stairs. He was younger than us, with short brown hair and looked a lot like Danny when he was younger.

"Go back to bed, Will," Alfred said.

"It's alright, Mr Squires," Danny said, taking my hand. "I'd better go home with them."

We walked to the open door and Danny turned back. "I'll see you again, Will. Thanks for everything, Mr Squires."

We followed Lizzie and future Danny across the road. I glanced back at Alfred Squires standing in his doorway with his hands in his trouser pockets, watching us.

"That's my great grandad," Danny said. "How mad is that. He died before I was born but I've actually met him now. And Will, my grandad, is eight years old. This time-shifting thing is totally amazing."

We were about to turn the corner into the next street when Danny let go of my hand and ran back to the house and hugged his great grandad.

Future Danny looked down at the pavement and wiped his eyes with the back of his hand.

"This is way too emotional," Lizzie said.

Alfred waited until Danny had rejoined us before he closed his front door. Future Danny slung his arm across Danny's shoulders. "Now, do you three think you can stay together until we get to Blackfriars Road?"

"What's at Blackfriars Road?" Danny asked.

"The way home," future Danny said as we set off again.

"You remember," I said. "It's the place where we can time-shift back to the 21st March 2012."

"Except," future Danny said, "you're not going to just time-shift to Blackfriars Road 2012, you're going to time-shift to Warwick Castle 21st March 2012."

"Yeah right, because we've done so well at time-shifting together so far," Lizzie said.

"I so don't miss you being little Miss Negative," future Danny said.

"I'm not negative," Lizzie said. "I'm a realist."

"You're negative," Danny, future Danny and me said together.

Lizzie huffed and stomped ahead.

"We need to turn right at the top of this road," future Danny called after her.

"Hold on," Danny said, grabbing my arm. "Where are your and Lizzie's future selves?"

"Time-shifting away the people from the future who are after us."

"Are they okay, you know, future Maisie and Lizzie?"

"I don't know. I hope so."

Lizzie was nearly at the end of the road and future Danny started jogging to catch up with her.

"You know when we were on London Bridge, I thought we were time-shifting to the cottage," Danny said.

"We were. I ended up there without you. I scared Lizzie stupid. She nearly hit me with a frying pan."

Danny stopped and grabbed my arm. "Did you hear a scream?"

Lizzie screamed again and future Danny

sprinted up the road and disappeared round the corner.

"Come on," Danny said, breaking into a run. I raced after him. The street in front of us was wide and a sign on the corner house said "Blackfriars Road". Further up on our right was a bridge over the glinting water of the Thames. Future Danny had hold of Lizzie and was pulling her back. I looked to the left and saw why. Maisie struggled against a heavily built man who had his arm gripped across her chest. Behind them another man held a knife to future Lizzie's throat, while their free hands were handcuffed together. I started to run towards them but future Danny caught hold of me too. "It's no good getting yourself captured."

"Danny, get them out of here!" Maisie screamed. The man holding her clamped his hand over her mouth. He roared as she bit it and then elbowed him in the ribs. He loosened his grip on her and she swung round and kicked him hard in the chest. He staggered back and she turned and ran towards us.

"Get them home," future Danny said, clasping the side of Maisie's face before charging forwards and rugby tackling the man to the ground before he could regain his balance.

"Those children even move," the man with the knife at future Lizzie's throat shouted, "I'll kill her!"

"No!" Lizzie screamed. She clutched at Maisie's sleeve. "We've got to do something."

"He won't hurt me!" future Lizzie shouted. "He knows I'm not worth anything dead."

The man hesitated before lowering the knife and headbutting future Lizzie instead. "We're going to get you. You can't hide forever!" he roared, dragging future Lizzie with him towards us.

Maisie turned to us, and with tears in her eyes she hugged me. "You need to go, it's too dangerous here."

"What about you?"

"As long as you three get home, everything will be fine. Trust me."

Future Lizzie struggled against the man she was handcuffed to and he couldn't move very far. The second man charged forwards knocking into future Danny, sending them both sprawling on to the road. I could hear the familiar drone of planes. I turned towards the Thames and caught sight of German bomber planes heading towards us.

"You need to go now," Maisie said, pushing me towards Danny and Lizzie. They both grabbed my hands. The rumble of the planes got louder.

The man fighting future Danny caught him off guard and with a kick to his ribs knocked him to the ground. The man turned and sprinted towards us.

"Run!" Maisie said.

So we ran, our legs pounding the tarmac of the empty road. I had no idea how close behind us the man was. We just kept going.

"Think about the castle!" Maisie shouted after

us. "Remember what it looked, smelt and felt like. Believe you're there!"

The roar of the fighter planes drowned her out. They were above us, ready to release their bombs over the dark city. I felt a hand grasp my ankle and I kicked my foot back as hard as I could. The road beneath us cracked. I focused on the castle and squeezed Danny's and Lizzie's hands tighter when my feet felt like they were pounding air. The heat, noise and darkness were sucked from around us. I couldn't see or feel anything.

My body jolted downwards. It felt like the sudden moment of waking in bed after dreaming about falling. My feet found solid ground and my back jarred against a stone wall. I opened my eyes. Lizzie stood opposite me on the narrow stairway of Warwick Castle's gaol.

"We did it," she said.

I looked up the stone steps lit by electric lights to the open trapdoor and daylight. "Where's Danny?"

Her smile faded. "He's disappeared again?"

A shiver down my spine made me shudder. "That man caught hold of me before we time-shifted. He could have got hold of Danny too."

We raced up the stone steps and emerged through the hatch at the base of the tower into daylight. The tree was there and the tented entrance to the dungeon. We crossed to the Great Hall steps so we could see the whole of the castle.

"Over by the tower," Lizzie pointed.

Surrounded by our class, Miss Chard was

ticking names off her list. I could see Adam Rickett and Lizzie's friends Josie and Megan, but no Danny.

"Of course!" I grabbed Lizzie's hand and pulled her towards the gatehouse.

"Maisie! Lizzie!" Miss Chard called as we ran past. "We've been waiting for you. Where are Nathan and Danny?"

"Give us a minute!"

"And what on earth are you wearing?" she called after us. "You know you're not supposed to have changed back into your own clothes until home time!"

"Our own clothes!" Lizzie said as we raced over the cobbles beneath the gatehouse. "She's seriously suggesting this skirt looks like something I'd choose to wear?"

"At least we're wearing 1940s clothes and not those stupid fifteenth-century dresses."

"Even so, we're in so much trouble."

"Not as much as we will be if we don't find Danny." We emerged from beneath the gatehouse on to the path that led past the rose garden to the castle entrance.

"No way." Lizzie tugged at my jumper sleeve. "Maisie, look."

I glanced to our left along the length of the castle wall to where two figures were rolling about in the grass. We ran towards them.

"It's my mobile," Danny said, pinning Nathan down in the grass. "Don't ever take it from me again."

"I'm sorry," Nathan sobbed, as he tried to struggle free.

"Danny, it's okay," I said, putting my hand on his shoulder. I felt him loosen his grip on Nathan and then he stood up, put his mobile in his pocket and brushed off the grass stuck to his knees.

Lizzie held her hand out to Nathan but he flinched away. She bit her lip and glanced at Danny and me. "I'm not going to hurt you," she said, taking hold of his hand and pulling him to his feet. Nathan looked really pale, like he'd seen a ghost. He glanced at Danny again and without saying a word he legged it back to the castle.

Danny grinned at us. "When we were running along Blackfriars Road I was thinking about chasing after Nathan and catching him and what I'd do to him, and I time-shifted right on top of him." He put his arms around Lizzie and me.

In the shadow of Warwick Castle the three of us, shouting and laughing, jumped up and down on the grassy slope. We were home.

If you enjoyed *Time Shifters: Into the Past*, then continue the adventure in...

Time Shifters: A Long Way From Home
&
Time Shifters: Out of Time

Available now!

THANK YOU TO...

I've always been fascinated by history and I wrote my first time travel novel when I was just eight years old. Fast-forward almost twenty years and the idea behind *Time Shifters* began in 2004 when I studied for my MA in Creative Writing at Bath Spa University. I took a course called Exploration and Experimentation and our tutor, Jonathan Neale, tasked the class with writing the first chapter of a completely different novel from the one we were already working on. A visit to Warwick Castle had sparked the idea for the setting and my desire, stemming from when I was young, to write an exciting adventure story that kids (and hopefully adults) would love, resulted in what would become the opening of *Time Shifters: Into the Past*.

Although writing is often considered a lonely occupation, it actually takes a great number of people to bring a novel to life. My thanks go of course to Jonathan Neale for his inspiring class that most certainly allowed me to explore and experiment with my writing and dream up Maisie, Danny and Lizzie and their adventures. There are also my brilliant beta readers, Judith van Dijkhuizen, Elaine Jeremiah, Debbie Young, Alana Terry, Emily Witt, Eden Mabee and her young son, Marcus, who not only said such lovely things about the book but came up with some incredible suggestions on how to make it stronger. Special thanks should go to Marcus for his honest and insightful feedback, and his soft spot for Lizzie! The cover was dreamt up and designed by the incredibly talented Rachel Lawston along with Robbie's map, and the fabulous Kate Haigh of Kateproof proofread the book. Last but not least I'm eternally grateful for the never-ending support of my mum and dad, the unwavering support and encouragement from my wonderful husband Nik, and the enthusiasm of my son Leo, my very own little adventurer.

JOIN THE TIME SHIFTERS!

This is where you need to tap your mum or dad, grandma or grandad on the shoulder, show them the book and ask if they can sign you up to the Time Shifters Club!

It's free to join, all that is needed is an email address (an adult's or yours if you have one) – simply go to www.kate-frost.co.uk, click on the *Time Shifters* tab at the top and then on the link where the email address can then be entered.

You will receive a free PDF filled with insider info about Maisie, Danny, Lizzie and the *Time Shifters* series that can be downloaded and printed out. Only occasional news about new books in the series or special offers will ever be emailed to whoever signs up.

If you enjoyed *Time Shifters: Into the Past* then please do tell all your friends about the book! Reviews on Amazon and/or Goodreads are always very welcome too (you can get an adult to write one on your behalf).

There are plenty more adventures to come for Maisie, Danny and Lizzie in *Time Shifters: A Long Way From Home* and *Time Shifters: Out of Time*. Both can be ordered online or at all good bookshops.

Thanks for reading!

Kate x

9 780995 478015